BUCKSKIN GIRL

When the half-Indian girl asked hired gun Walker Strett for his help to track down her father's killers, he agreed. What he didn't know was that the murder took place eleven years ago, but if he was in any doubt about how serious Cherokee was in her quest, he could just ask the man whose kneecaps she shot out, before finally killing him. Strett had seen things that would make an Apache blanch — but he'd never seen anything quite like this buckskin girl . . .

Books by Tyler Hatch
in the Linford Western Library:

A LAND TO DIE FOR

TYLER HATCH

◆

BUCKSKIN GIRL

Complete and Unabridged

LINFORD
Leicester

1999 by

First Linford Edition
published 2000
by arrangement with
Robert Hale Limited
London

The moral right of the author
has been asserted

British Library CIP Data

Hatch, Tyler
    Buckskin girl.—Large print ed.—
Linford western library
1. Western stories
2. Large type books
I. Title
823.9′14 [F]

ISBN 0–7089–5797–8

Published by
F. A. Thorpe (Publishing)
Anstey, Leicestershire
Set by Words & Graphics Ltd.
Anstey, Leicestershire
Printed and bound in Great Britain by
T. J. International Ltd., Padstow, Cornwall

This book is printed on acid-free paper

1

Execution

Idaho was the first to arrive. He thought the place looked like it hadn't been visited in twenty years.

No, not quite, he amended silently. Almost exactly *eleven* years since the Werewolves had met and planned and then left for what they figured was going to be the biggest job of their lives.

'Christ!' he said aloud. 'Eleven goddamn *years*!'

It really didn't look all that different. He folded his hands on the saddle horn and stared down the length of the hidden canyon. Part of the cabin's roof had caved in, the door sagged, and a window was propped open on a stick just as it had been the last time he was here. Could it be the same stick? he

1

wondered. What the hell did it matter, anyway?

'Might as well go on down and get the place into some kind of shape before the others come,' he murmured, straightening, stiff from the long ride. Then added pessimistically, '*If* they come . . . '

He kicked his heels into the weary dun's flanks, edging it down the slope from the grassy bench. He felt kind of exposed, riding in across the flats. In the old days, no one would be able to do that unless they had passed muster with the guard hidden on the rim. Even so, they would still have been under the gun of someone at one of the windows. The only way their gang had survived for so long was because they took such belt-and-braces precautions.

Halfway to the cabin, Idaho knew he had made a near fatal mistake.

A shot crashed at the same time as gravel kicked up bare inches in front of the dun's forefeet. The horse whinnied and jerked its head, beginning to rear.

Idaho fought it down, using one hand to make a wild grab for his six-gun, but froze when a second bullet whipped air above his head. He remembered the procedure then, halted, straightened a little and lifted his hands head-high.

'It's Idaho Reese!' he called.

Silence, except for the dying echoes of the gunfire. Then a voice he didn't recognize called calmly, 'Come on in just as you are, hands high — one twitch and you'll find out if there is life after death!'

Damned if he recognized that grating voice!

But Idaho did as he was ordered, heart still hammering from the shock of the gunfire — and he was mad at himself for being so damn loco as to take it for granted that no one was in the cabin — just because he hadn't seen any tracks.

Whoever it was must have gotten his horse out of sight, likely around the back in that brush-choked little draw they used — which could mean it was one of the old bunch — no one else would know about that draw.

But he was through taking chances today, squared his rounded shoulders and blinked, eyes watering some, feeling gritty under the lids. Hell, *that* could be why he hadn't noticed any tracks! The sawbones at the penitentiary had warned him he ought to have his eyes examined when he got out.

'You've got excess pressure building in the left eye, Idaho. It could mean glaucoma which will eventually send you blind if left untreated. I can give you the name of a good man in St Louis . . . '

'Doc, when I get out, I won't be goin' anywheres near St Louis. And don't worry none about my eyesight: I can see just as good as ever. Good enough for what I aim to do, leastways. After that . . . ' He shrugged his round shoulders.

'You didn't let me finish,' the kindly old doctor said. 'You have the beginning of a cataract in your right eye. The prognosis for your continued normal sight is not good, Idaho, I'm afraid. Be sensible, go see about it when you leave here.'

Of course he hadn't. He had been released only days after the doctor's final examination and he had put in a lot of travelling since, covering many miles before finally coming here for the rendezvous, right on the deadline, by his figuring.

But, if he *had* missed seeing sign of an intruder, or even one of the old bunch when coming in, well, maybe he ought to consult someone about his eyes. The prospect of blindness left a shaft of ice in his chest, but this chore had to be done first!

At all costs. Even the cost of losing his sight . . .

'By God, it *is* you, Idaho!'

The voice startled him out of his reverie and he saw that the dun had reached the clump of trees surrounding the cabin. Light flashed briefly from a rifle barrel at the window with the propped-up shutter and he halted the horse. He had no time to decide whether he was going to make a grab for his six-gun, for the man holding the rifle stepped out of the cabin.

Idaho Reese thought he saw a flash of teeth through the heavy beard and moustache. The nose was almost flattened and one eye had a droopy lid traced with thread-like scars. The left ear appeared as if it might have been clawed up by a bear or a wolf, but he could still recognize French Pete Lucas. And yet — that voice, gravelly, strained, not at all like the loud, gusty tones that he remembered . . .

'Pete?' Idaho's narrow face was very wary, the eyes slitted, the stooped shoulders stiff with tension.

'You bet!' French Pete laughed, limping forward, dragging his left leg a little. He stopped beside the dun, grinned, and held up a broken-knuckled hand.

Idaho gripped with him: the strength of those thick fingers wrapping round his hand was the way he recollected, anyway. Like that last handshake before the posse drove the whole gang to scatter, every man for himself.

Inside the cabin, at the old table French Pete had set up, one sagging leg resting on a rock, Idaho swigged from the stone jug of whiskey Pete produced and wiped his mouth on his grimy sleeve. He was unable to keep from staring at the other man.

'The hell happened, Pete?'

The bearded man was seated on a tree-stump stool — Idaho recalled The Canuck had made that — rubbing absently at his thigh. He grimaced as he shrugged.

'Son of a bitch of a warder named Sanchez happened, that's what.' He pulled down his neckerchief and Idaho for the first time saw the twisted scars there. 'Hit me with a rock-drill, almost killed me. Crushed part of my voice-box which explains why I talk the way I do now.'

Idaho took another swig at the hooch.

'What happened to Sanchez?' He knew *something* would have — Pete and he had been the ones who never forgave a hurt, always squared-away with anyone loco enough to cross them . . .

Pete grinned. 'Sanchez had an accident, a real bad one — just before I was due for release. Shame it was. Rock shelf collapsed on him, buried him alive. Took 'em five hours to dig him out, screamin' all the time. He held out for a week, then died.'

Idaho smiled thinly. 'Debt paid in the best Werewolf tradition, eh, Pete?' He threw back his head, howled briefly.

'Damn right!' Pete sobered now. 'Just the way we square away with McKenna.'

'By hell, yeah!' Idaho glanced through the window. 'Looks like it might be up to just you an' me.'

'Aw, there's a coupla days to the deadline.'

Idaho looked surprised. 'Yeah? What day is it?'

'Sunday, twenty-third. We set it for

the twenty-fifth, remember?'

'Ah I thought today *was* the twenty-fifth. Well, hope someone else shows. Want to swap experiences over a few more drinks?'

French Pete shook his head, tapped his temple. 'Got it all up here, every blamed minute I spent in that lousy pen. I don't need to talk about it. But you go ahead, if you want. I'm still a good listener.'

Idaho Reese shrugged. 'Heard they hung Salty over to Yuma.'

'Nah, that was just talk. He was lucky, mind. They had him headed for the gallows but some do-gooders kicked up a fuss, complained that because he was crippled, he'd paid enough for his crimes. Kept at the judge until he cut Salty's sentence to twenty years.'

'Hell's own luck, eh! Well, he always was lucky, or that buckshot charge woulda tore his guts out. Still, he won't be here . . . '

Pete smiled crookedly. 'Don't bet on it.'

'What? Twenty years, you said . . . '

'Sure. But he's out.'

'How the hell! Not many escape from Yuma . . . '

'Nah, nah. Told you there was some do-gooders watchin' out for him. Damn if one of the women don't fall for him — he was always good-lookin', ol' Salt, you recollect. Anyways, she married him and somehow got the governor to parole him in her care.'

'Well, I'll be! Guess Salty ain't lost none of his sweet-talkin' ways.'

Pete chuckled. 'Yeah. Dunno how his wife's takin' it, but he got word to me he'll be here.'

'Well, that's good news. Anyone else you know for sure is comin'?'

Pete drank deeply, belched and handed the jug back to Idaho. 'Brock'll be here. Ran into him on a chain gang workin' Rainbow Pass for that new railroad. He wasn't due out for a month after me but he reckoned he could get here in time.'

'Then that only leaves The Canuck.'

'Yeah. Last I heard of him, he was real pissed. Said he come down to the States to make his fortune an' had no intention of goin' back to that widder-woman he fancied up in Manitoba with nothin' in his pockets. But he said he'll get this chore done with us first.'

Idaho tensed. 'Do I detect a hint there that might mean there's a . . . job comin' up afterwards?'

French Pete laughed outright, a wheezing, half-coughing sound. He slapped his left thigh, winced a little, threw back his head and howled like a wolf — just like in the old days when spirits ran high and they were young enough to feel the sap singing through their veins.

'Got me a beauty in my sights, Idaho! Heard about it by accident from a stage-company guard they threw into my cell while he was waitin' sentence for bein' tied into a hold-up. Idaho, old pard, if we can nail McKenna and then pull off this one last job — man, we'll be sittin' pretty! All five of us.'

11

It sounded good, but there was just a faint fluttering deep down in Idaho's belly.

Sure, there were five of them, but Red McKenna was one tough son of a bitch and even after all these years he'd be mighty leery and on the look-out for them.

Even if they got to him it didn't mean all five of them would ride away from it.

That was the kind of ornery bastard McKenna was.

★ ★ ★

McKenna walked down to the river, carrying his Winchester rifle as usual. He stood on the high bank and looked around him as was his normal habit, taking in the river flats, the distant cabin with the faint curl of blue smoke rising from the rusted chimney. He sighed, pale-blue gaze resting on that cabin.

He'd always figured that by this

stage of his life he would have a big ranch house with riverstone fireplace large enough to roast an ox in. Green pastures spilling away to the horizon, blanketed with red, black and brindle cattle. *His* cattle . . .

He shook his head and shaggy, rust-coloured hair swirled about his shoulders. *No use gettin' into that now . . . Rose was long gone.* Irritably, he tugged at the collarless flannel shirt, pulling it away from his neck, turned and stomped on down to the part of the river he had been working for months now. He had built a rocking-box, complete with water-chute and riffles, had even managed to find a few small nuggets. Their edges were jagged and rough, which meant they hadn't been washed too far from their source. He hadn't dared hope there might be a mother lode upstream, but he was gradually working his way up there — and still finding small, rough-edged nuggets.

He had a hunch he was getting closer.

Hell, it was time his luck changed for the better! He decided to walk up that way, dive down into the deeper pools, see if he could find a pocket of nuggets lurking there. He picked up his sack of tools and excitement knotted his belly, despite his attempts to keep it from overwhelming him. He looked back once more at the cabin. He could see it from here where the river-bank sloped down easy and shallow to the water's edge.

Maybe it wasn't yet too late to dream of that big ranch house and his own herds of cattle. Sure, Rose was gone but there was —

He let the sack of tools drop with a clatter, snatched the rifle across his chest and levered a shell into the breech.

Across the river, a buckboard rumbled out of the trees and turned down to the ford, slowing, allowing the team to slake their thirst. The driver was a black man and he had a sun-faded Navajo blanket draped across his legs.

The reins were knotted about his left hand, his right holding the handbrake lever.

'Oh. Good mornin' to you, sir! Didn't realize I was close to civilization.' The Negro waved briefly, in friendly manner. 'Trust I'm not trespassing, sir?'

McKenna frowned. *Did he know that voice?* Ah, he'd have to stop jumping at his own shadow this way. These days there were plenty of Negroes who drove buckboards, even fringe-top surreys, having made their fortunes just after the war. Anyway, he'd heard the man he was thinking of had been hanged in Yuma, nigh on ten years ago now.

'This land is mine. Mebbe it ain't deeded in my name, but I use it.' As he spoke, McKenna squinted, trying to get a good look at the man's face which was shaded by the wide brim of his hat. 'I guess you can water your team.'

'Obliged, sir. Making my way to Rapid City. Some 'helpful' white man — with a somewhat twisted sense of

15

humour, I suspect — told me there was a short cut across the Badlands, even drew me a map marking the waterholes. Of course they'd been dry for years. So I did what I used to do when I was a kid and stayed out till darkness caught me in the woods — I picked a star I liked and followed it, and it brought me here. I slept in my buckboard yonder, behind those trees, and now . . . '

McKenna started to bring up his rifle and the man stopped talking abruptly. 'I don't believe in ghosts, mister!'

The man seemed startled. 'Well, sir, I don't know what prompted that remark, but — Please! Would you mind pointing that rifle elsewhere? I mean you no harm. My own gun is in the back, with my camping gear — and my crutches.'

McKenna, feeling a little foolish, yet still somehow shaken, held the rifle tightly, not lowering it. Images flew through his brain — blurred by the years and gunsmoke.

'You — you just be on your way. Your team's watered now!'

'Well, it is my intention to continue my journey, sir,' the man said, making no move to lift his reins or release the brake handle. 'I just don't know why you are so put out with me, of a sudden.'

Goddamnit! thought McKenna, sweating a little now. It couldn't be him! Burns never spoke like this — he was nothin' more than a swamp-runnin' Nigger, never had been, never would be.

Then he whirled, sensing rather than hearing something behind him. He froze when he saw the two horsemen, one on the high bank, the other now between him and the cabin. Then he whirled to his left as a twig cracked and another silent rider appeared at the edge of the brush. A fifth man showed himself at a clump of rocks some yards ahead of the Negro, neatly cutting off McKenna's escape across the ford. And the driver reached under

17

his Navajo blanket and produced a sawn-off shotgun.

Gun hammers clicked all around McKenna. He felt dizzy as he spun his head this way and that, trapped by these men.

Then his blood ran cold as they suddenly howled like a pack of wolves.

His legs almost gave way beneath him as the Negro smiled coldly and said, 'Yes, you were right to be suspicious of me, Red — but I'm no ghost. They didn't hang me and I've come to settle with you. With a little help from my friends. I'm sure you don't need to be introduced.'

McKenna was shaking helplessly now. He didn't even have enough strength left to pull the trigger of the rifle. He simply stood there with the river lapping his old boots, staring into gun muzzles whichever way he turned.

'How — how'd you find me?' he croaked.

'Wasn't easy, Red,' Idaho Reese told

him. 'But we invested a little time and money — not our own, as you'll savvy. Took us a spell but now — *here we are*, you son of a bitch!'

French Pete rubbed gently at his scarred throat, staring bleakly at the red-haired man. The Canuck, a beefy man with short, thick legs and a darkish face, hawked and spat on McKenna's stained old work-shirt.

Brock, a square-faced, beard-stubbled man with mean eyes, sat his mount on the high bank and growled impatiently, 'The hell're we wastin' time on talk for? It was all said nigh on twelve years ago — *all* said! Now it's time to finish it!' He glanced at his companions. 'Werewolves — are you ready?'

'Yeah!' snapped Idaho, lifting his rifle. 'Let's get it done!'

McKenna stirred at last. He plunged into the river, slipping, shooting wildly, levering as fast as he could, heading for deeper water where a swift current flowed. French Pete spurred his horse ahead of McKenna, turning him with a bullet that zipped into the water right alongside the desperate man's leg.

McKenna stumbled, reared up, levering as he spun, not knowing which way to shoot as the riders surged in towards him. Then their guns thundered in ragged volley that tore the morning's peace apart and McKenna's shredded body jerked and twisted, briefly lashed the river to bloody foam before flopping face down, edged away by the relentless tug of the current.

'Damn!' swore Idaho, looking surprised as well as annoyed. 'I think I missed!'

'Don't much matter, does it?' the Canuck growled, watching the bleeding corpse slowly floating downstream.

Then Idaho put his horse alongside McKenna and fired two bullets into the corpse, sinking it briefly, although it bobbed to the surface and started drifting again.

'*Now* I feel better!' Reese said.

The others said nothing, not surprised at this demonstration of Idaho's mean streak. Then the Negro snapped his head up, staring at the distant cabin.

'What?' queried Brock who was closest to him.

'Thought I heard a cry — maybe a child . . . '

'Likely a bird disturbed by that Greener of yours,' allowed French Pete. 'What we gonna do about the cabin? I doubt we'll find any *dinero* there.'

'Burn it,' snapped Idaho and the others agreed.

'Well, you gents go ahead,' the Negro, Burns, said. 'I guess I've done what I came to do.' He glanced towards the corpse that was floating into the bend by now.

'You ain't joinin' us, Salt?' Pete asked. 'On that other deal, I mean?'

Burns smiled sadly. 'I'm a married man now, Pete. Happily so. My wife is an understanding woman and she gave me her blessing to come do this. Now I'm obligated to return to her and take care of her.'

'Well, good luck, Salt,' the Canuck said. 'She must be some woman. Sure taught you to talk real pretty, anyways.'

'Why thank you, Canuck, thank you kindly. I wish you gennlemen all the best and if you're ever passing through Red Oak, Iowa, well, come look me up. You'll be welcome.' He smiled thinly as he looked at them one by one. 'I guess from this moment on, the Werewolves are now officially disbanded, eh?'

He turned the buckboard and drove back towards the trees, lifting a hand in farewell without looking back.

'Now there goes one lucky man,' Idaho said a mite wistfully — or was it enviously?

'Yeah. He made it good. With a little help,' agreed Brock.

'Mebbe we can do it, too,' Pete said, but they only stared at him until they started riding up towards the cabin and the Canuck said, 'Quit kiddin' yourself, Pete. The likes of us won't never make it amongst ordinary folk — and I ain't even sure I want to.'

But no one commented. Minutes later, the cabin was ablaze.

2

Gun For Hire

The town was mighty busy when Walker Strett rode in on his trail-dusted bay gelding. Wagons and buck-boards and riders seemed to be cutting across each other in all directions.

Strett kneed the bay this way and that, holding the reins in one hand, right hand resting on his thigh. He rode tall in the saddle, shoulders square and wide, the old smoke-smelling canvas jacket hanging from them loosely. His hat was battered and greasy-marked from his long hair, matted in back of his head and hanging over his frayed collar. The rest of his clothes were sun-faded and worn, but beneath the dust, his boots were of good quality, as was the leather gunbelt and the Colt that rested snugly in the tied-down holster.

He looked at some of the paint-peeling signs as he rode on through the crowds, wondering what made this place so attractive to so many people. Likely because it was a railhead, he decided, for he couldn't figure anything else that would bring in such a population. The buildings were mostly timber, a few brick ones scattered here and there. There was nothing to look at — the town was slap-bang in the middle of grey, uninteresting flats. The real scenery didn't start for many miles and from here the ranges were just a low, purple-blue mark wandering across the horizon.

But he hadn't come to look at the scenery and he didn't aim to stop over for long. Just get the chore done and be on his way. With a little luck . . .

The law office fronted Main between a general store and a saddler's. It looked kind of squeezed but he could see down the narrow alley that it ran a good way back in a long, narrow building. Looked to him like there would be a good-sized cell-block in there. Well, with a railhead town and trail crews cutting loose when they were paid off, he figured there would need to be plenty of cells.

And it would take a tough man to enforce the town ordinance and throw any curly-wolves behind bars.

He rode the bay up to the hitch rail and dismounted stiffly, looping the rein ends over the hickory before using his hat to slap dust from his clothes. He coughed a little, took off his neckerchief and wiped his face with it. As it passed across his eyes, he became aware of the man now standing in the doorway of the law office.

He looked lean and mean, his clothes of good-enough quality, but the sawn-off shotgun he held with polished barrels, engraved receiver, and checkered pistol grip, was of the very best quality. It was pointing to the ground right now, but Strett could see the tension in the thick wrist, ready to swing the gun up in an instant.

Cold green eyes studied him and the sheriff spurted a stream of tobacco juice accurately across the boardwalk into the gutter: Strett figured it wasn't the first time he'd done it.

He nodded civilly to the lawman. 'Howdy, Sheriff. Like a word with you if you've got a minute.'

The man continued to chew, spat another short stream of juice and stood to one side, beckoning with the Greener. Strett hesitated briefly, watching the gun as he moved into the dim office. It was sparsely furnished but the desk was good wood, cherry-maple he thought, waxed and clean of chips and scratches. There were few papers on it, but a leather-and-silver humidor stood in the middle nearest Strett and a pad and pencil, neatly aligned, were to the left. He had noticed that the sheriff held the shotgun in his left hand, also. The man stepped past Strett behind the desk where a good quality buff Stetson hung on a peg, a neatly pleated woollen jacket beside it. The sheriff sat down and Strett pushed back his hat, dropped into the chair on his side.

The lawman glared. 'I invite you to sit?'

Strett arched his eyebrows. 'Sure I heard you do so, Sheriff.'

The man's narrow face scowled. 'Don't get smart with me, Strett!' He spat his tobacco plug into a wastebin with a *clang*.

Strett tensed. So-oooo — he was *that* kind of sheriff . . . kept up with the Wanted dodgers and hired guns.

'Well, I'll dust off the seat before I go,' Strett said easily. 'Need a little information.'

'Needing it don't mean you'll get it.'

'What's the burr under you, Sheriff? I've only just arrived in town.'

'And I want to see you riding out just as fast as that crowbait at the hitch rail can take you.'

'My business oughtn't to take long — just want some directions, if you don't mind.'

The lawman said nothing and Strett shrugged, started to reach for the makings before he remembered he had run out of tobacco a few days earlier.

'Three men. I hear they're either in or around this town — Luke Magill, Johnny Booker and Hunter Cole. Can you tell me where I'll find 'em?'

'Why?'

'Got business with 'em.'

The sheriff curled a lip. 'Someone hire you to gun 'em down?'

'Whatever my business is with them, Sheriff, I'll keep it outside of your town. That suit you?'

'Nothing you do or say suits me, Strett! Your kind gripe my guts . . . damn paid killers, nothing less!'

Strett sighed, fumbled in the dusty pocket of his shirt, brought out a sweat-darkened leather folder and took a paper from it. He pushed it across the desk. The sheriff reluctantly glanced at it, but didn't touch the paper. His lean body stiffened slightly and his eyes narrowed.

'Wells, Fargo . . . ?'

'Uh-huh. The gents I mentioned relieved the Socorro stage of some seventeen thousand dollars a coupla months back . . . I've been on their trail for six weeks and it led me here.'

He could see the Wells, Fargo official warrant paper had thrown the hostile lawman. It must have fair twisted his bowels in a knot to know he *had* to help Strett whether he liked it or not now . . . Wells, Fargo was no one to mess with.

He eased back in his chair, the Greener still in his lap, cold eyes watching Strett's stubbled, wolfish face.

'They work for a man named Hank Greener.' He slapped the shotgun and added, deadpan, 'No relation. The spread's ten miles north, through the Boone River Pass. You'll see a signpost at a fork in the trail . . . ' He stopped, but seemed as if he had more to say so Strett waited. 'You need a hand? I could spare a deputy . . . '

Strett stood, shaking his head.

'Thanks, no.' He picked up his Wells, Fargo warrant and put it back in his pocket. 'Obliged, Sheriff. I'll tend to my horse and my own needs, then I'll be out of your hair.'

'And keep it that way — I don't like hired killers in my town, Strett, no matter who they work for.'

Strett nodded, used his neckerchief to dust off the seat of the chair and stepped outside. When he led his weary bay through the doors of the livery across the street, he saw that the lawman was back in the doorway — minus the Greener now — staring in his direction coldly.

He was still there a couple of hours later when Strett rode out, bathed and barbered and fed, the horse having been given oats and a rub down at the livery. Strett made a point of flicking the sheriff a salute but the man didn't even scowl, just stared with hostility.

It didn't bother Strett. Long ago he had grown used to hostile lawmen and others who didn't care for his profession.

Some called him 'manhunter', most just plain 'hired killer'.

It didn't bother him. Not any more.

★ ★ ★

The pass was a death trap.

That was Strett's first thought when he saw it. High-walled, narrow, the steep slopes dotted with clumps of brush and boulders. He recalled there had been a massacre here during the war that rivalled the slaughter at Glorietta Pass.

He was on the edge of a butte, a mile from the pass, and he already had the feeling that it could well prove to be his personal Boot Hill. He had survived a long time as a freelance gun-for-hire, not a little because he had generally followed his hunches. They had started during the war when he had been part of a group called Ryback's Rangers, scouts who infiltrated enemy

31

lines well in advance of their own men. Several times, reacting to those hunches had saved his neck and those of his men. Since the war ended, the same premonitions had brought him safely through several sticky situations.

Strett pursed his lips in thought, rolled a cigarette from the new sack of tobacco he had bought in town and smoked it down, resting in the afternoon shade of a huge boulder on the north face of the butte.

By the time he had finished, he knew just what he was going to do.

If anyone was waiting in the pass for him as he suspected, they wouldn't have seen him yet. And he made sure any watching eyes didn't see him ease down from that butte by taking a trail down the east face. It was risky, and twice the bay slid and raised a small dustcloud. But at the bottom, he was in the deep, almost black shadow of the butte. As the sun sank lower in the sky, the shadow lengthened and darkened. He used it, circled down into a dry wash he had noticed from higher up, and dismounted before he reached the end. He was now only a couple of hundred yards from the entrance to the pass and he carried his rifle, spare shells in his jacket pockets.

Crouching, he dashed from rock to rock, dropped into a small arroyo, snugged down in a bend beneath a jutting cutbank. Within minutes, he knew he had been right to follow his hunch . . .

The setting sun was blazing its last red-gold rays into the pass itself, lighting one wall like a huge fire, the ruddy light reflecting to also illuminate the opposite wall.

And to flash off metal halfway up the slope behind a bush as a man moved restlessly, careless how he held his rifle.

One. His narrowed, sky-blue eyes, searched that slope carefully, pinpointed another man almost at the same level, but deeper into the pass. *Two*. His gaze shifted to the other wall, now looking like molten gold — and throwing the shadow of a man crouched amongst smooth round rocks, his hat and upright rifle barrel stretched out distortedly, but a plain warning for a man like Strett. *Three.* That should be it, but . . .

Four! Damn, he almost missed the fourth man, who was up on the rim, now squirming a little to look down into the pass. His voice reached Strett.

'Hank! Hank! He ain't gonna show now. Whyn't we go on back to the spread? If he's loco enough to come tonight, we can easily take care of him.'

'Whyn't you shut up!' Hank Greener called in a strained whisper. 'Lefty's man said he'd be leavin' town in plenty of time to reach the pass by sundown. We wait. Now get back under cover, you blamed idiot!'

The man on the rim slid back out of sight and Strett was already moving. He crept away from the cutbank, hugging the deep shadows, worked his way onto the slope of the mountain bisected by the pass. Below him spread the wide expanse of the Boone River, hissing and gurgling over a pebbled bottom here, dropping into minor rapids. All its sounds helped cover Strett's progress as he climbed the slope, unworried that he would be seen now.

Near the top, he crouched double, pushed back his hat and let it hang down his back by the tie-thong. He caught a whiff of the bay rum the barber had sprinkled on his newly cut hair back in town, raised his head slowly.

The small breeze that had brought him the scent of his hair, suddenly reversed and blew towards the man lying prone on the broken rim of the pass. As he eased his way over the top, Strett swore silently when the man lifted his head and he heard him sniffing. That damn bay rum!

He lunged forward just as the man twisted around, glimpsed the whites of widening, startled eyes, heard the grunt of effort as the man rolled on to his back and tried to bring his rifle up. Strett stooped quickly, grabbed the man's boots and upended him with a violent heave.

The bushwhacker screamed as he went over the edge and Strett knew the others' eyes would be glued to that failing body instinctively. He dropped prone in the same spot where the man had lain, felt the warmth of the earth through his clothes, and brought his rifle to his shoulder.

He saw the body hit down there, the small explosion of dust and gravel, and then the sliding of the limp-limbed corpse. One man on the opposite wall had exposed himself thoughtlessly as he half-rose to see his partner strike the bottom of the pass. Strett shot him, saw him jerk upright, smashed him down with a second shot.

He immediately swung the rifle down-slope to where he had seen the sun strike the gun barrel amongst the brush, raked it with three fast shots.

The brush jerked and a man tumbled into view, sliding and rolling down the slope.

Stones kicked into Strett's face, cutting his cheek, forcing him to jerk back. But not before he had glimpsed the man below, Hank Greener. He had moved fast, slipping out from behind the rocks that had hidden him from below, to the opposite side of the boulders, still using them for cover as he fired at the rim.

Strett rolled and slid several yards to his right, clawed himself up to the edge, but before he could get his rifle up, Greener had him spotted. The man's bullet puffed dust against Strett's throat before whining away in a savage ricochet. Strett swore: this ranny knew his business. He dropped flat, but Hank Greener didn't waste his lead on him.

Strett moved further to his right and as he worked to the edge again, heard rocks clattering. He heaved himself half upright, rifle coming up, saw Greener leaping wildly down the slope, stumbling, hurrying into the shelter of more boulders, rifle held out to one side to help his balance. Strett fired twice, narrowly missing with both shots, and so emptied his magazine.

He lay on his side, hurriedly fumbling fresh shells from his jacket pocket, swiftly pushing them through the loading-gate into the tubular magazine. By then Hank Greener had disappeared into the rocks and the sundown shadows filled the pass, giving him extra cover. Strett leapt up and started running down the slope. He hadn't known if Greener had been part of the stage hold-up with the other three or not, but now it seemed clear the rancher must have been.

Strett heard Greener's horse clattering away through the narrow end of the pass even before he reached his ground-hitched bay and vaulted into the saddle. It was a lousy time to be in pursuit of a desperate, ruthless man, but he had to run him down swiftly or lose him altogether.

He thundered through the pass, glimpsing the bodies of the two men he had shot. One might have had a little life left in him, he thought, but he kept riding, wrenching the bay's reins to the left as he reached the end of the pass.

Then, racing between two high rocks there came a swift, brief hiss and he glimpsed something rising towards him at blurring speed. He tried to wheel the bay and duck at the same time, but the taut rope caught him across the chest and next thing he was catapulting through the air backwards. The breath had been wrenched from his lungs and he fought to hold on to his rifle, body twisting in mid-air.

He smashed into the dark ground, lights bursting behind his eyes, felt the rifle skid from his grip. He was still rolling when he had the impression of a horse leaping forward from behind a rock and, on the edge of oblivion, thought, Here's where it ends, feller — thirty-eight years old and you're about to die by a stage-robber's gun in this Godforsaken part of Nevada . . . and all because of your own carelessness . . .

Then he had the impression of the horse leaping over him and dust blinded him, grit stinging his face and filling his open mouth. A paroxysm of coughing brought him back from the threatened oblivion and when it was over, his ears roaring, he clawed grit from his eyes.

He blinked. A rider had his bay's reins in one hand and was racing away with the gelding alongside his own mount. But it wasn't Hank Greener.

It was a fiery-haired woman dressed in buckskin.

3

Buckskin Girl

The bay was tied to a bush in a gulch cut by a shallow creek with sparse grass growing along the bank.

Weary, battered, barely able to see in the fast-fading light, Walker Strett stumbled up the gulch to the animal and leaned against its shoulder. It nuzzled him in recognition and he felt its belly. It had grazed the grass and no doubt drunk its fill. He rammed his rifle into the scabbard, leaning against the horse. He wouldn't be able to ride the bay at any speed for a while now without risking its health, maybe its life.

Sighing, he drank at the creek, rolled a smoke, still not quite sure of what had happened to him. Had it been a dream? *Was* that really a woman in buckskin who had knocked him out of his saddle with the rope and then taken his horse?

Well, seemed she hadn't meant him too much harm. Just aimed to delay him — and now had even left him his horse where it could get to water and feed.

So who the hell was she and what part did she play in this? Friend of Hank Greener's, that's who she was. Had to be. Slowed him down and gave Greener a chance to vamoose.

He frowned. But would a man like Greener just keep running under such circumstances? No, he'd be more likely to come back and put a bullet through Strett's head while he was down and helpless.

Maybe not — ah, the hell with it. His head throbbed too much to try to figure it now. He had hit his head hard on the ground, had gravel scars down one side of his face, a lump above one ear so that he had to wear his hat tilted to the opposite side.

Worst of all was the lousy taste in his mouth — not caused by the dust he had swallowed, or anything he had eaten or even the creek water. No, it was there because Greener had gotten away, would be miles into the hills by now, thanks to that damn buckskin gal . . .

But he was wrong about that.

After he had finished the cigarette, he mounted the bay and walked it across the creek. There was a quarter-moon and he could see tracks. Seemed she hadn't taken the time to hide them, which meant she didn't care whether he found them or not.

He followed them for an hour, twisting and climbing, dropping down to lower levels, and, in a dead-end canyon he found Hank Greener.

The man was dead, but he hadn't died easily. Both his knee caps had been shot away. There was blood and marks in the soft soil to show how he had crawled frantically this way and that, terrified of . . . something.

Three bullets had finished him. Two in the chest. One through the head. An assassin's way of making certain . . .

And all over the place were the tracks of the horse ridden by the woman in buckskin.

He shook his head, started to mount the bay, when he noticed some splashes of blood on a rock that didn't fit the pattern of the others. It wasn't Hank Greener's blood, he was sure of that: the dying man's sign went nowhere near that rock.

Frowning, unshipping his Colt, he made his way afoot into the rocks, seeing more dark splashes. His foot turned on a stone and he swore softly at the noise he made as he groped swiftly for a grip.

Flame stabbed out of the blackness ahead and he dropped swiftly but awkwardly as a bullet ricocheted from the rock where he had his hand. He rolled onto his side, fired a wild shot, rolled back the other way as the hidden rifle blasted again. The shot was really wild this time and although his instinct was to shoot at the muzzle flash, he held back and in the silence after the echoes died away, he thought he heard a small sound like a moan and then a clatter, as if someone had dropped a gun.

Taking a chance, trying not to get any pale rocks at his back, he clambered forward on to the top of a boulder and then he saw the dark figure lying sprawled on the sand between two rocks. The rifle had fallen to the ground and the moonlight reflected from the shoulder-length chestnut hair with the deep glow of live embers.

She had a hand pressed into her left side, holding some sort of bloody cloth against the wound. He stood up and she heard him, stiffened, snapped her head up, must have seen him against the stars. She sobbed and made a lunge for the fallen rifle and he jumped down, stumbled, but managed to plant a boot on the barrel before she could pick up the weapon.

'Easy! I'm not going to hurt you.'

Her face was a pale blur, almost featureless in the shadow of her hat which was askew on her head. But he saw the flash of bared teeth and thought the eyes glinted a little. She said nothing and he stooped, lifted her rifle and placed it up on top of a rock at head height. Then he holstered his six-gun and knelt beside her, reaching for the wound in her side.

'He got one good shot in, huh?'

She writhed and tried to push him away with her bloody hand — and then he saw the other hand swinging at him, something she held in it glinting in a streak of moonlight.

The point of the blade just caught his jacket sleeve as he threw himself backwards and he heard the canvas rip. Then he slapped the hand aside, twisted the knife free. It had a strange heft to it and he glanced down at it.

A short, crudely shaped blade with a deer horn handle wrapped partly in

46

rawhide. An Indian knife . . .

He tossed it up with the rifle, spoke harshly to her.

'Look, you're bleeding like a turkey bound for Thanksgiving dinner. Let me see if I can stop it. I already told you I ain't gonna hurt you.'

'You try and — I'll — kill you!'

He smiled crookedly. 'I don't doubt you'll try. Who are you?'

Of course she didn't answer, and he stood, walked away and began to climb over the boulders.

'Where . . . where're you . . . going?' she called anxiously, words edged with her pain.

'To my horse. To get my canteen and some clean rags.'

He didn't wait to hear any reply she might have made, returned in a few minutes. He soaked a clean rag in water and gently mopped at the wound: she had pulled up the bullet-torn buckskin overshirt while he had been away. The bullet had sliced the flesh over her ribs and she winced, jerked, bit back a sob as he felt the ribs.

'Bruised, but I don't think anything's broken. It'd be better if the water was hot and I could heat a blade to cauterize this.'

'It ought to be safe to light a fire . . . now,' she told him, sounding short of breath. 'You killed the other three . . . '

He looked at her sharply. 'But you wanted Greener for yourself.'

She said nothing and he gathered some twigs and deadwood jammed in the rocks by past thaws, when the creek had swollen and its waters had reached up to here. She watched him closely in the firelight, studying his face, and he, in turn got a better look at her.

Her skin was a kind of matt gold and her eyes were deep and brown, the nose slightly aquiline, the cheek bones a little more prominent than most. *Indian blood*, he figured.

'You're law?' she asked, as he set water heating, took his own honed knife blade and set it beside the flames.

'No. Hired gun. Wells, Fargo, right now.'

She nodded. 'The Socorro stage hold-up. You must be very good to find them.'

'Three of them. I didn't know about Greener till I hit that pass at Boone River.'

'Yes — he was the brains behind it. They used his ranch as a hideout . . . and his name wasn't Greener.'

Strett arched his eyebrows, tested the blade. 'Be ready in a moment or two. Bite on this strip of harness leather.'

She took it and placed it between her teeth and he saw that now her features were more composed — resigned, like an Indian's, ready to face the oncoming pain as stoically as possible.

The heat from the glowing blade seared his face as he held it up.

'What was his real name?' he asked, using the question as a diversion so that when she said 'Brock' he pressed the red-hot metal along the edges of the wound and she made strangled sounds and the ends of the thick harness leather rose as she bit down. Sweat coursed down her face and her breath hissed through the pinched nostrils and then her eyes rolled up so that he glimpsed the whites just before she fainted. He leaned across her. She had a wild smell about her.

He worked swiftly and had the wound cleansed and an iodine-soaked cotton pad bound over it before she made the first signs of coming round.

He gave her some cool water and she almost choked on the first mouthful, took the next more slowly. She looked up into his wolf-like face only inches from hers.

'I think I've seen you . . . before. In Laredo . . . Two years ago — '

'I was there at that time. Name's Walker Strett.'

He felt her stiffen slightly. 'The gunfighter-for-hire.' There was no contempt in her voice as there was when most folk were told his identity.

50

Just stating a fact.

'And you are . . . ?' he urged.

'My name won't mean anything to you . . . '

'Maybe not, but I'd like to know it anyway.'

She was silent for so long he thought she had passed out again and he was actually lowering her gently to the ground when suddenly she said, 'I'm Cherokee McKenna.'

The last syllable trailed off as she slipped into unconsciousness once more.

★ ★ ★

The birds calling amongst the trees along the creek bank woke Strett to the grey, pink-and-lavender colours of dawn. The sun was not yet in sight above the ridge but the sky was lightening by the minute.

He was stiff and his head still throbbed, thin scabs already forming on the gravel scars on his sore face.

51

He scrubbed a hand around his jaw, hearing the rasp of the stubble just barely rising above his skin. He paused halfway through the motion, looked across the small grassy clearing to where he had made a bed of boughs for the girl in the bloodstained buckskins.

She had thrown off the blankets he had draped over her last night and now hugged herself in the coolness of early morning. She was still asleep and muttered something unintelligible, as he rose and rearranged the blankets over her. He knelt, lifted one edge, pushed up the buckskin shirt a ways and examined the flesh around the wound beneath the bandage. From what he could see it didn't look to be inflamed and that was a good thing.

The camp-fire was going within minutes and he set coffee to heating and hacked some fatback from the cheesecloth-wrapped slab in his grub-sack. The skillet was sizzling with melting grease as he laid the strips of meat in it. He turned them with his knife, but they were barely singed when a voice spoke behind him.

'So, this is what happened to you.'

He turned quickly, hand instinctively going back towards his gun butt, but he froze the movement when he saw the Greener with the polished barrels covering him.

The sheriff held it ready to shoot and he had back-up in the shape of a queer-looking ranny, rail-thin, his eyes not only on different levels but of different colours, one blue, one brown. The man had a mean twist to his mouth and his over-sized right hand held a cocked six-gun.

Strett remained crouched by the fire, turned the fatback again. 'Was going to come back and see you, Sheriff.'

'Sure you were — and bring in all them dead men back in the pass. And Greener himself in that dead-end canyon. You've had yourself a mighty busy time since last I saw you, Strett. Who's the woman?'

'Stranger. Stopped some stray lead

fired by Greener.'

The lawman grunted. The deputy looked meaner than ever.

'Why you shoot-up Hank that away?'

Strett remained silent, not yet having any ready explanation for the way Greener's kneecaps had been blasted to splinters.

'I wish I'd stayed with the others in the pass!' the deputy said sourly. 'He wouldn't be cookin' no fatback right now.'

Strett flicked his eyes to the sheriff. 'Lefty — that what they call you?' Even before the sheriff stiffened, Strett knew he was right, remembering the set-up on the lawman's desk that favoured the left-hand side, and now seeing the way he held the shotgun, left hand on the pistol grip. 'Sure — Lefty. You sent a man on ahead to warn Greener and the other three while I was having my horse groomed and getting myself cleaned-up in town.'

'Watch your mouth, Strett!'

Strett smiled thinly. 'You were in it,

weren't you? Let them operate from here for a share of the loot.'

'You're talkin' yourself into a six-foot slab of Nevada, mister!'

'Maybe. I saw those filing cabinets with the labels on the doors, all nice and neat. One read 'Wanted Dodgers'. You'd have seen Brock on at least one. He's been wanted for years all through the southwest. Even tried to track him myself once . . . '

'Who the hell's Brock?'

'Greener, you know that. You and your deputy were part of it.'

He turned to the bacon, lifted several pieces out on to a tin plate.

'Watch out!'

He didn't actually recognize the girl's weak voice until later, but he reacted swiftly. He scooped the skillet of bubbling grease around in a short arc and it fanned into the crooked face of the deputy. The man screamed and his noise and violent staggering threw the sheriff's aim off. The charge in the shotgun blasted the fire all over the clearing, but by then Strett was diving headlong, rolling several times, wrenching around even as the lawman cocked the Greener's second hammer. The six-gun barked twice and the sheriff staggered, lurched into the sobbing deputy. He fell to one knee, tried to bring up the shotgun but couldn't make it. He spread out on his face and then the deputy at last remembered the Colt he still held in one hand, turned a raw, blistered face towards Strett and triggered a wild shot. Strett pushed up to his knees as the deputy fired again, the lead whipping past his face. Then he shot the man and the skinny frame jerked and collapsed so fast Strett wondered what had happened — it was like air going out of a burst balloon.

The campsite was hazed with gun-smoke and his ears were ringing with the thunderclap of the guns as he crossed quickly to the girl. She was propped up on one elbow, pale, staring up at him with those big brown eyes.

'*Ayieee!* I — I've never seen — You

are so very fast!' she whispered.

'Had to be. Obliged for the warning. I didn't think he'd try anything right then . . . How's the wound?'

'Sore and stiff. But what will you do now . . . ? These two were lawmen. You killed them. How can you prove Brock was paying them off? *We* know, but — ' She shrugged and grimaced.

He went on reloading his six-gun, spun the cylinder and dropped the weapon back into his holster.

'You're likely right there. I'll rig things to make it look like the sheriff and his deputy shot it out with Brock and his men. They'll be heroes, even if they won't know it. Even being dead heroes is too good for 'em. But . . . '

She frowned slightly and he thought how handsome a woman she was. Barely a woman, he figured. She couldn't be more than twenty. Young, healthy — and pretty damn ruthless judging by the way she had disposed of Brock. She interested him but he figured it would be some time before she told him anything about herself. She had an independent look about her.

'I'll cook some more breakfast and then tend to your wound. It needs bathing several times a day. You want me to take you to a sawbones in town?'

'No!' The reply was swift and emphatic. As he arched his eyebrows, she looked away and added, 'I — have things to do. I can't afford time in an infirmary with some frontier quack fussing over me.'

He gathered wood for another fire, got it going, cut more bacon and set up the coffee and skillet again.

'You're way tougher than any gal I've ever known and I've knowed some *real* tough ones in my time.'

She stared at him but said nothing. He tended the frying bacon and asked, 'How'd you come by a name like 'Cherokee'?'

A long silence and just when he had decided she wasn't going to answer, she said, 'My mother was half-Cherokee.

I didn't care much for my name, but I liked 'Cherokee', so I took it — because of her, I suppose. Her name was Rosebud.'

'She's dead?'

She nodded, lips tightening a little. 'I don't remember her. She died when I was very young. My father and . . . another woman reared me.'

'The other woman a squaw?'

Her hands clenched. 'She was an Indian woman, yes! 'Squaw' is not in any Indian language. It's a white man's word.'

'You're right. But I meant no disrespect when I used it. I was once called 'Squaw Man' some years back.'

Her gaze sharpened. 'That's what they used to call my father before — Well, he's dead now, too.'

He asked if she wanted some bacon and at first she refused, but then changed her mind, so he fried up some cornpone in the grease and dished up a plate of food for her. She drank her coffee down first and held out the mug for a refill. After he complied, she began to eat and he sat on a fallen tree a few feet from her blanket roll, eating with his knife.

'You go and live with the Indians after your father died?'

She snapped her head up. 'How did you . . . ? Why would you ask such a thing?'

He shrugged. 'Indians could teach you to be tough the way you are, able to stand pain that would throw any white woman into a fit of heebie-jeebies.'

She ate on, then murmured, 'You learn to be as tough as the other women, or you are treated badly.'

He nodded. 'The Indian way. Part of their survival code. The weak can only bring down the tribe. Like Nature they sort out the wheat from the chaff.'

She almost smiled. 'You have a strange way of talking — or perhaps it's that I still tend to think in Comanche and then translate it into English.'

His face was sober. 'You must've been with them a long time for that to happen!'

'Yes. Over ten years. I almost forgot how to speak English . . . Why do you look at me like that?'

He started a little, pushed the last strip of fatback into his mouth. 'Sorry. Was just thinking. The Comanche can be a wild and cruel people, but they can also show a heap of kindness to children. 'Specially female children, who can grow up to bear sons to strengthen the tribe . . . '

She pushed her empty plate away, lifted the coffee mug in both hands and used it to cover her face while she sipped slowly. It was some time before she lowered the mug and saw he was still looking steadily at her.

'In answer to the question you have not yet asked, Yes, I married a buck and he was a fine man, a brave warrior.'

'Was?'

She nodded. 'He died protecting the camp in a raid by white soldiers. The woman who was living with my father and who took me to her tribe, she was killed at the same time. Her sister is looking after my son.'

Her jaw tilted and her eyes flashed challengingly, daring him to say something. He did, but perhaps not quite what she was expecting.

'Then something mighty powerful must have brought you all this way just to kill Brock.'

The surprise was clear on her face. 'You — are you part-Indian? Do you have a *shaman* somewhere amongst your ancestors?' He shook his head, smiling, and she added, 'It's very strange how you can put your finger on things so . . . so well.'

'Just logic, Cherokee. Brock have anything to do with the death of your husband and the woman who took you to the Comanche?'

She shook her head. 'Not my husband's nor Sun Flower's death, no.'

He rolled a cigarette and had it half

smoked before he stiffened suddenly and snapped his gaze towards her where she was sitting up, slowly unravelling the bandage from around her wound.

'By God! Brock killed your father? Eleven *years* back . . . ?'

The brown eyes met and held his unwaveringly. 'He was one of the men who did it.'

Strett blew out a long plume of tobacco smoke. 'You sure have a long memory!'

'Indians never forget a wrong done to them by a white man.'

'So I've heard,' he acknowledged slowly. 'But you said Brock was only *one* of your father's killers?'

'Yes. There were five of them. He knew they would come for him one day and he left a letter for me with Sun Flower long before his death. Amongst other things it said, 'if ever I am murdered, look for these five men.' And he listed their names.'

'Kind of strange . . . '

'No, it's not. He was asking me to

avenge his death; now I am able to. My obligations to the tribe have reached a point where I can spend time searching for my father's killers.'

She meant it, he could see that. 'A long, cold trail, Cherokee.'

'I have time.'

'You're doing it alone?'

She hesitated. 'I started out that way. It took me many months to find Brock . . . I know I owe you my life.'

'You squared that a little time back warning me about the sheriff.'

'No, you tended my wound. I . . . maybe I bleed to death if you don't. This is a big thing you do for me, but still must ask — it is too much, maybe, but I ask will you help me find the other men who killed my father? Teach me how to use a gun properly and I'll do the rest. Will you, Walker Strett? Please?'

'Begging don't suit you!' he said curtly. He noticed that her speech became less fluent, more stilted, with excitement.

Her head tilted. 'I will do anything I have to to avenge my father. Beg, steal, kill, *anything*!'

'This Brock — he tell you where to find the others?'

She sobered, dropped her gaze. 'No. He died before I could ask him.'

Strett smiled crookedly. 'Lucky Brock, I'd say.'

She stared defiantly. 'I'll do anything I have to, I said . . . I mean it.'

'Yeah — guess you do. Look, it must've been pure luck you found Brock after all this time.'

'No. I work hard, spend Comanche gold, and eventually I found him.' Her face changed subtly. 'You are interested in gold, aren't you?'

'Man's got to eat — why? You offering to pay me some?'

'Of course. I would not expect you to give me your time for nothing. Aren't you, after all, a hired gun?'

This time there was a touch of contempt in the way she said it and it surprised him when he felt a wrench in his chest. Hell, he hadn't cared a good goddamn for many years what folk thought about the way he made his living. Way he looked at it, gunfighting was the best talent he had so why not exploit it?

'Not by you,' he said flatly, and surprised himself once more. 'Folk seem to die all around you, Cherokee: I don't have the hankerin' to join 'em.'

She frowned. 'I do not understand. Why do you refuse gold when you are a bounty hunter?'

'Might as well call me a wolf-hunter — I run a trapline in the Jerichos some winters.'

'Yes, that is good wolf country.'

He lifted one eyebrow. 'You've been there?'

'The tribe wintered there once.'

He snapped his fingers. 'By hell, then we almost met before this. I recollect a bunch of Comanche wintering on the big sand bar at the salt bend of the Jericho River a few years back.'

'Ah! You were *that* wolf-hunter! You

were all hair and so buried in your buffalo robe that we could not tell just *what* you were! Yes, I saw you. My son had just been born and it was a sunny day and they had lifted the skirts of my teepee so I could get fresh air . . . '

He sobered. 'Makes no difference. I can't help you.'

'Why? Because I am part Indian and I want to kill white men?'

He wiped that away with a cutting motion of his hand. 'I'm working for Wells, Fargo . . . I have to report on this job, try to recover some of the payroll Brock and his pards took.'

'So you can claim a reward? I will pay you more.'

'Why me?'

'You are fast, gunfighter, can teach me how to kill my enemies. It is good, the way you think, like arranging things here to make it look like a battle between lawmen and outlaws. You are a man-hunter and . . . I need your help.'

He tapped his fingers against his gun butt.

'I *must* do this thing, Walker Strett!'

Yeah, he could see that. But did he really want to help her?

4

Recovery

Strett saddled his horse but left the girl's grazing and ground-hitched. She lay on her blankets, watching him closely.

'I'll go set things in order for that shoot-out that never was and then I'll go through the pass and see if I can find Brock's spread. I need to recover some of that payroll money. Or try to.'

'You will not know where to look.'

He shrugged. 'I've found over the years that most folk tend to hide things around a house in pretty much the same places. I've got to try: I owe it to Wells, Fargo. You'll be OK here. There's water and grub within reach. Don't move around too much or that wound's gonna burst open and start bleeding again.'

She was very sober now since he had not yet made any reply to her request for his help in tracking down the killers of her father. He had decided he would need to know a lot more about it and, truth was, he wasn't very keen to get involved.

He swung aboard the bay, touched a hand to his hatbrim and rode back to the clump of boulders where the sheriff and his deputy had tried to jump him.

The girl watched him go in silence, unsmiling . . .

★ ★ ★

He took the bodies, slung across their mounts which he found in a small draw close by, back to the pass where the other dead men were still scattered about.

It wasn't a pleasant job arranging them in positions that would look as if the lawmen had been ambushed but had given a good account of themselves in the ensuing fight.

After all, the bodies had lain in the open all night and half the day and there were clouds of flies — and some had been visited by hungry animals.

But he set the tableau to his satisfaction, searched for and rounded-up all the horses again, then drove them down to the creek and the grass, turning them loose.

He was sweating in the early afternoon, drank from the cool creek and sluiced water over his head and upper body. Then he put his shirt on while he was still wet, rode through the pass and found the fork in the road with its weathered sign pointing the way to 'Greener's Slash G'.

It was a ranch too small for a four-man crew: merely a cabin with a lean-to for extra bunks, a shaded area of the corrals for feeding the mounts and a crude blacksmith's forge against one side of a winter hay shed.

Strett saw a few cows dotting the slopes of the hogback which rose behind the buildings and protected them from the bitter winter winds. No, anyone with any experience would see that this was a blind, a fake ranch, near the Boone River Pass that would provide fast exit to the wilds of west Utah, and the hills only a frog's leap away.

The cabin was untidy and smelled of stale food and cooking grease and man-sweat. The lean-to, strangely, was quite neat and he figured the two men who had slept here took some pride in where they lived.

He found some of the stolen payroll stashed in the bottom of a coffee can in the main cabin, more of it rammed up into a hollow bunk support. The good old hearth stone hideaway proved to contain a small wooden cigar box crammed with money, a withered rabbit's foot and an old Sharps buffalo cartridge in tarnished and verdigrised case with a white oxide formed on the huge lead bullet. He turned up a couple of silver dollars between the roof support and shingles at the rear of the cabin, a small cache above the door. The lean-to provided money tied into the tail of a dirty shirt tossed carelessly into a drawer, as if ready for laundering.

All in all he recovered just under $10,000. He counted it roughly, tied it up in the same dirty shirt and crammed it down to the bottom of his saddle-bags.

He would have to find a town with a Wells, Fargo agency where he could deposit this.

It was a successful mission and he ended it by burning the cabin, releasing the horses in the corral, then rode back to the camp where he had left Cherokee McKenna.

It was just dark when he arrived and he missed the place at first, but realized he was too far upstream, rode down the creek and came out into the camp from that direction.

The girl had gone. She had taken her blankets and rifle and half his food. There was a small deer-hide drawstring poke resting in a prominent place on a rock beside the dead fire where he couldn't fail to see it.

Inside were three small nuggets of gold.

Well, he thought as he gathered wood for his cooking fire, he no longer had to decide whether he was going to help her or not: she'd made the decision for him.

★ ★ ★

There was a town along the main trail through the Boone River pass and while it didn't have a Wells, Fargo agency, it had a bank that Wells, Fargo Express Company had an interest in. He deposited the recovered payroll, got his receipt and sent a telegraph to head office putting them in the picture.

He asked around, hoping to find some trace of the girl, telling himself he only wanted to make sure she was all right and had had enough good sense to go to a doctor. But no one had seen her and her dun horse was not in the livery and the doctor said no one answering her description had called on him.

Strett shrugged and went to the saloon, ate an over-salted meal that took four large beers to wash down. By the time he had finished the meal he had decided to 'just check' that she had made it safely out of the Boone River country . . .

It meant starting back at the campsite by the creek. He found her tracks easily but later, amongst some timber, he saw where she had made an attempt to cover them. Did pretty good, too, but she was bleeding again, judging by the dark splashes he found in the vicinity.

Twice more, once on the far side of a stream, and another on top of a ridge, he found where she had tried to cover her tracks.

There were more and bigger dark splashes now and he increased his pace, pausing on the ridgetop only to figure out what direction she might have taken.

Logically, she would stay where there was readily available water, so that meant she would be heading north-west, maybe making for the Virgin River across in Utah. He had no idea where she might be going, but she was sure moving away from civilization. Maybe she knew of some Indians in these parts, though they were a long way from Comanche territory.

He found himself growing anxious as the day wore on and he hadn't yet sighted her. When the sun went down and he had found no more sign of her he started to really worry.

He spent a sleepless night, only closing his eyes a couple of hours before sun-up after he had decided he must have missed her trail coming down from that big ridge.

He rode there fast next morning, chewing on jerky and washing it down with canteen water by way of breakfast. Halfway up the slope he dismounted and half an hour later found where she had turned aside from the descent, very carefully riding in close to a big deadfall that screened most of her tracks. When he had passed they would have been in the log's deep shadow . . . but he found them this time.

They led him across the face of the slope, turned up-grade again into a jutting buttress of granite with a pile of huge broken boulders at its base.

There was a cave, of course, and her horse, scenting the bay, whinnied and led him directly to it.

The dun was still saddled, reins weighted with a rock and there were signs that showed she had more or less fallen from the saddle.

'Cherokee?' he called, voice coming back hollowly to him.

There was no answer and he went in warily, hand on six-gun, turned quickly to his left when he heard an animal sound.

But it was no animal: it was Cherokee McKenna, huddled in a shivering, yet sweating position on the piled blankets. They looked as if she had torn them from her bedroll, didn't have enough strength to spread them properly and had collapsed upon them.

Her buckskin shirt and trousers were stiff with blood and her flesh was swollen and purple around the split-open wound he saw when he examined it.

She raved in fever, speaking in a language he decided was Comanche, recognizing one or two words.

The first thing he did was start a fire and set a pan of water heating.

While it did so, he made her a proper bed, cutting brush from amongst the boulders outside, stripped off her clothes and covered her with the blankets.

He heated his knife blade for he was going to have to lance the wound and release the pus and infection.

After it was done and she had cried out several times, he bound it tightly halfway up her rib-cage, covered her shivering body, adding his own blankets to the pile, then slid down the slope until he found a stream. He scraped willowbark with his knife blade, found a bird's nest at the edge of a clump of cattails — likely a wild duck's — and took the eggs back to the cave.

The willow, infused with hot water in a tin mug, he fed to her throughout the day and night and by the following morning her fever had broken.

He cleansed and redressed the wound and tended to the horses.

Then found he was ravenous, not having eaten all day, made himself some supper and fell asleep against the hard rock wall. He woke once during the night, stiff and store, crawled to the girl's bed, and found she was sleeping normally, breathing steadily, her brow only slightly warm to his touch. He forced another infusion of willowbark on her and then made a rough bed from the saddle-bags and emptied grubsacks and went to sleep.

It took three days before Cherokee

showed any real signs of being on the road to recovery. By that time the wound was almost completely drained of infection and the purple had faded and the flesh was returning to its normal healthy matt-gold colour.

She didn't say much, watched with those large brown eyes as he moved about the cave, making food or coffee for her, going down to the nearby creek to rinse the blankets. Her buckskin outfit was already washed clean of blood and dirt and he brought it inside from where he had draped it over a bush, folded it neatly and dropped it on the ground beside her.

'You might feel better if you put your outfit on.' He spoke more gruffly than he meant to.

'Why? It bothers you that I am naked under this blanket?'

'Not me, Cherokee.'

'Well, it . . . it doesn't bother me either!' She didn't sound convincing and he said nothing. 'I mean — well, I know you must have washed me all over many times during the fever. It would be stupid of me to feel embarrassed now.'

'Sure. It would be stupid because it was a chore that needed to be done and there was no one else here but me to do it. You're beautiful, Cherokee, but sickness kills desire.'

She flushed despite her attempt at an uncaring attitude and he lifted a hand as she began to stammer a reply.

'You need a few more days a'bed, then a few more taking it easy while you get back on your feet literally. You're lucky the bullet bounced off your ribs without splintering them.'

'I think I am lucky that you came back to look for me.'

'Well, I guess that's right — and you needn't have left those gold nuggets for the food.'

She lowered her eyes but said nothing. After he had a meal cooking she said, 'I am hungry now — that is a good sign, I think.'

'Yeah. I've got some more eggs for

an omelette for you.'

After a while, watching him prepare the meal, she said, 'My father was an outlaw.'

He snapped his head up. 'I wondered . . . '

'Oh, it was a long time ago, before I was born. He told me about it when I was old enough to understand. He rode with those five men he named as his killers. Something happened on some big robbery they pulled. I don't know what it was . . . but they came all together, even one man, a black man, in a buckboard because he was a cripple. And they killed my father!'

Strett frowned, thinking they sure must have wanted to kill McKenna real bad . . .

'They trapped my father down at the river, got between him and the cabin. I saw it all from the cabin window and I think I screamed when they shot him but Sun Flower clapped a hand over my mouth and took me away from there very fast. It was just as well, too.

The men came up from the river — all howling like wolves — and burned the cabin and corrals and scattered my father's few cattle into the hills.'

Strett concentrated on the cooking. Some kind of savage hatred had made those men do that. Whatever McKenna had done to them must have been mighty bad.

'Sun Flower took me to the Indian camp and they kept me there. After a while I stopped trying to run away, realized I had nowhere else to go, that there was no one in the world left for me to turn to except Sun Flower and the tribe.'

'How old were you?'

'Nine or ten, I'm not sure. I don't know why the men murdered my father, but he was a kind man, very good to me and to Sun Flower. He cared for injured animals I brought home from the wild. He worked hard and I never went hungry even if there wasn't enough food for him or Sun Flower. He was *good*, Walker Strett, and he did not deserve to die at the hands of those men. Now I will see that they die badly, too.'

He glanced up. 'Well, you've got the background for that.'

She stiffened but saw that he was not being insulting. She nodded. 'Yes, I think that is why I put it off for so many years. I used my pregnancy and marriage, the caring for my son, as excuses, but I think although I *wanted* to avenge my father, I didn't quite have enough courage to do it, even though I knew how to go about it. You can not live for so long with Comanches and not learn how to kill . . . Then one day about six months ago, I knew it was time and so . . . ' She spread her hands. 'Here I am.'

'With one notch already carved on your gun.'

She frowned. 'I do not carve notches.'

'Just talking, Cherokee. I meant you've already nailed Brock. You know where to find these other men?'

Cherokee McKenna shook her head.

'I have a vague idea where one man may be — I am hoping you will help me. You have had experience hunting men . . . a lot of experience. What will you take for your reward?'

He stirred the omelette, threw a handful of crushed beans into the coffee pot and dusted off his hands before looking her squarely in the face and saying, 'Nothing.'

Her frown deepened. 'You won't help me?'

'Oh, I'll help you all right, but I'll want to be sure the men we hunt down are the right men and as bad as you make out. If they are, then they need killing.'

She almost smiled. '*Then* we will kill them!'

He nodded gently. 'Yeah. If they're as bad as you say, we'll kill them.'

'One by one!' Her eyes were glinting with excitement now. 'Until we have them all!'

'You're kinda blood-thirsty, aren't you?' He gave her a crooked smile but she was sober now.

'No. I just keep remembering how my father's body was torn apart by that hail of bullets, how he fell into the river like — like nothing more than a bundle of rags.'

Strett poured the coffee silently, thinking that that must have been one hell of an image for any young girl to carry in her head for eleven years.

5

Manhunt

It was a long ride to the Wasatch Mountains in Utah.

When the girl told him she had a vague clue that that was where one of the killers was, Strett insisted she lay up at the camp for another week.

'I can show you something about guns in that time, so it won't be wasted,' he told her when she objected. 'But you need to make sure you're strong enough for a ride like that.'

'You forget, I have been living with the Comanche. They are great horsemen. I have ridden many miles, walked many more . . . I am stronger than you think.'

'Could be. But a few extra days won't hurt. Anyway, what makes you think this feller is holed-up in the Wasatch?'

She looked a little dubious. 'It was just something I heard while I was looking for Brock. My lead to him was strongest so I didn't follow up the other. I was working for my keep in a saloon that also served meals, in Durango, Colorado.'

'The Dollar's Edge?' Strett asked and she looked surprised.

'Yes. You know many saloons, I think.'

'Goes with the job — but . . . ?'

She continued. 'I was serving a table of trail men on their way through the San Juan Mountains. They had been drinking and were laughing and joking and one man mentioned a whorehouse in a town called Wheeler's Falls on the lower reaches of the Green River. He spoke of its attractions and said it was run by a man who called himself the Count. But the cowboy had known him years earlier in prison and then he was called French Pete.' She looked at Strett steadily. 'That was one of the names on the list my father left — French Pete Lucas.'

Strett drew on his cigarette. 'Cherokee, I wouldn't mind a dollar for every feller with the nickname of French Pete I've come across over the years. Or 'French' something or other.'

She nodded soberly. 'I know, but it is possible it is the same man because my father had added to his list that all the men on it were serving long gaol sentences at the time he wrote it out.'

'Still drawing a long bow.' At her frown of puzzlement he said, 'It's a mighty long shot that it's the same man.'

Her mouth tightened. 'But I have nothing else! I *must* follow it through. If only I had been able to catch Brock earlier, I would have made him talk!'

Strett admitted it *was* the only clue she had and that they might as well check it out.

Cherokee brightened. 'Meantime, you

will show me how to shoot properly.'
She went to one of her saddle-bags
and brought out a triangular cloth bag
that was a corner cut from a flour sack
and drawn together at the top with a
cord. Inside was an old Colt Army
cap-and-ball revolver in .44 calibre.
The blueing had worn through on
the cylinder and part of the barrel
from years of travelling in a holster,
but he found that the mechanism had
been oiled heavily in an attempt to
keep rust away.

'It was my father's . . . I have his
powder flask, a tin of wads and another
of percussion caps, as well as a supply
of lead balls. I would like to learn how
to use this gun.'

'To kill the men who murdered
him?'

Her eyes narrowed slightly. 'It would
be — I can not recall the right
word . . . '

'Appropriate,' he said. 'You oil this?'
She nodded and he shook his head
slowly. 'First thing we have to do is

take it apart and clean it. Then I'll tune it as well as I can, but I don't know if we can trust those percussion caps and powder.'

'Maybe we can buy more. We must try! I *must* use this gun to help avenge my father.'

'I'll get it working for you,' he promised, checking it over. 'The gun's free of rust. It'll take a little time, that's all ... you damn well *are* a blood-thirsty little thing!'

She didn't smile in return. 'When I need to be.'

★ ★ ★

Even after cleaning, the pistol was stiff and the cylinder hard to turn and she had to use both hands to cock it. Strett worked on it with files he took from a small tool kit in a chamois roll he kept in his saddle-bags.

He set to work, concentrating, not answering when she spoke to him. It was noon on the third day before he had it in working order again. They went to a draw where he set up pieces of branches on a deadfall, went through the laborious process of loading the cylinders with powder, ball and grease-smeared patch, chamber by chamber. Then he started to 'shoot it in'.

The gun had a good heft to it and although he was dubious about the reliability of the old percussion caps, those he fitted to the cylinder's nipples fired without hesitation. There was a good kick to the gun and he knew he would have to reduce the powder load for the girl. It was far from accurate, but as most six-guns were used within a few feet of a man-target, he reckoned she would bring down her victim.

It took some time to adjust the brass ball foresight and to file the notched rear sight more symmetrically, but it helped. She fired the gun held in both hands and he let her do this at first, so as to get used to the weapon. But then he insisted she used only one hand. She found it very awkward.

They spent two days in the draw, peppering the deadfall, and he dug out the distorted lead balls from the soft wood, telling her he would melt them down for re-use, casting them in the brass mould that she had among the accessories for the pistol.

She wasn't a natural good shot but she worked hard at increasing her accuracy and he knew she would be all right when — if — it ever became necessary to use the pistol in anger.

She had a lot of willingness going for her and that was the secret of being a good lawman or a good gunfighter, or a good soldier: the *willingness* to kill when needed.

At the end of the first day's ride she almost fell from the saddle, looked sallow and drawn around the mouth. Not that she had complained. In fact, she had berated him when he had slowed the pace.

'Don't be so damn impatient,

Cherokee. You've waited over ten years. Another day or two won't matter. Not if it makes the difference between arriving in good shape and having to spend a few days a'bed recuperating before you can go hunting for this French Pete.'

'You are *too* logical, Walker Strett!' she snapped at him, but she said nothing more when he didn't increase the new pace.

Wheeler's Falls was a lively place. They could tell that even before they reached it. There were herds of cattle bedded down on the riverside flats and a distant crackle like fireworks on the Fourth of July.

'Trailherders cutting loose in town,' he explained, when she looked at him quizzically. She squinted at the blurred buildings.

'There is no law here to worry about?'

'There'll be a sheriff or a town marshal. By the sounds of things, I'd say he isn't too zealous about keeping a tight lid on the trail men.'

'The whorehouse will be busy.'

He looked at her sharply. 'There'll be a bar — I can ask around without alerting this 'Count'.'

She smiled faintly. 'Perhaps I can do better.'

'What?' The idea startled him. 'Hell, you better keep right away from there until I find out something.'

'I will apply for a job. That way I will get to meet this French Pete.'

'You're crazy! You can't do that!'

'Why not? Am I not attractive enough?'

'It's not that — you know damn well just how attractive you are . . . '

'You know, too,' she replied mischievously.

'Yeah, well, I mean, they'll want to put you to work right away. Once those gal-crazy trail hands get a look at you, they won't want the usual sloppy, hard-headed women who work in those places. You won't get a chance to get out once you're in!'

'You seem to know a lot about whorehouses.'

'Damnit, I'm a man and I've hazed my share of cows up and down the trails to railhead in my time. Yeah, I do know what I'm talking about. So you leave this to me.'

She said nothing.

'You hear me? I want your word on this. Tell me you won't do anything stupid like applying for a job there. For Chris'sake, woman give me your word on it!'

She smiled crookedly. 'No. I will not tell you that. But I will wait until you see what you can find out. Then, if it is not enough . . . '

'If it's not enough, I'll try something else, but you stay right away from that place, hear?'

She sighed heavily. 'I hear. If you speak much louder, they'll hear you in the town, too.'

He nodded jerkily: he hadn't been aware he had been shouting, but the very idea of what she had proposed enraged him. Stupid damn woman! She'd get herself killed if she wasn't careful . . .

As they approached the town, skirting the herd now, she said quietly, 'I am not afraid to work in a whorehouse if it will help me find my father's killers. I told you I will do anything I have to.'

'Well, this is something you don't have to do. Just leave it to me.'

He wanted her to say 'yes', she would leave it to him, but she said nothing at all and he didn't like that stubborn look on her face.

Maybe she was going to cause more trouble than he could handle, he thought miserably.

He tried to book a couple of rooms, but in both cases the proprietors said they did not take Indians. She took it blandly, adding, teasingly, 'I'll bet they wouldn't say that at the Count's place.'

He knew she was right. 'Must be the buckskin. Maybe you better go buy yourself a dress.'

'No. I will not try to be what I am

not. I find buckskin comfortable. I will see to the horses in the livery and go to the saddler's for a holster for the pistol while you visit the Count.'

So that was the arrangement and Walker Strett found the bar of the 'Count's Pleasure Palace' packed with sweaty cowboys, some drunk, others sleeping on the floor in quiet corners, or with their heads down on their arms at the tables. It was a compact room, hung with velvet curtains and nude paintings. The place was noisy yet orderly, watched over by hard-eyed men on high stools. Strett ordered a beer and was jostled roughly by a trailman.

'Sorry, *amigo*,' the cowboy drawled, turning back to his conversation with his companion.

'That's the first Texas drawl I've heard in months,' Strett said, and the cowboy looked at him over his shoulder. Strett half-smiled, nodding civilly. 'I'm from San Angelo on the Concho.'

'I know where it is, for Chris'sakes,' growled the ranny, hard-eyed, sun-blackened and smelling strongly of the trail. He deliberately turned his back on Strett.

Strett touched him on the arm and the man snapped around irritably. 'Friend, this is my first time here,' Strett said amiably. 'Someone steered me here but I can see it's so damn crowded a man's gonna have to wait till sundown before he gets any lovin'. You boys know of anywhere else in town?'

The ranny lost some of his belligerent look. 'This is the only place. The Count's got the monopoly.'

'He really a count?'

'Hell, I dunno. Nor care. But he runs a fine string of women . . . '

Strett saw the man was going to turn away again and said quickly, 'Buy you a drink?'

'Buy one for my pard, too, and you got a deal. From San Angelo, huh? I'm from Amarillo. Bud Tesser. This here's Rowdy — call him that 'cause he don't hardly speak. Kinda shy. He's from — Arizona, ain't it, Rowdy?'

The other man, thick bodied, bearded, merely shook his head. Strett waited, but he didn't offer the name of the state he came from. Then the drinks arrived and they discussed trailherding and women and finally Strett turned it around to the Count again. By that time, he had bought three more rounds.

'Someone said he was French,' Strett offered.

'Well, heard a feller call him Frenchy now I think of it,' Tesser admitted, some of his words a trifle slurred now. 'But then I heard another feller call him Pete once, too. Count had his bouncer throw him out a top-floor window.'

'Sounds like he's got a past.'

Bud Tesser snorted, swaying a little. 'Ain't everyone?'

'Guess so . . . Was an outlaw a few years back called himself French Pete — Lucas, I think, though it was pronounced Loo-car. They say that's the French way.'

Tesser laughed. 'Ain't the French way I'm interested in!' He guffawed and banged his glass down on the wet bar top. 'Barkeep, fill 'er up an' send my pard Walker the bill, OK?' When the scowling 'keep obeyed and Strett paid, Tesser leaned closer to the man. 'Hey, your boss, he really an outlaw called French Pete? How you say you pronounce that name, Walker? Aw, yeah — Loo-*car*! Huh . . . ? That right, barkeep?'

The barkeep gave the Texan a hard look and moved away. Strett tensed, watching as he went to the beaded curtain that hung in a doorway at the far end of the bar. He spoke to someone out of sight, but then a man's hand parted the strings of beads. He looked down to the small group. Apparently the booze had loosened Rowdy's tongue for he and Bud Tesser were leaning into each other, starting to sing a trail ditty whose words would not have been allowed outside of a place like the Pleasure Palace.

Strett pretended to join in but he was watching the curtained doorway. The man the barkeep had spoken to was visible now, tall, wide-shouldered, gun-hung, his clothes a little better than most men's in the bar, but not flamboyant like a gambler's. Just better quality and cut. He was clean-shaven except for a thin moustache on his upper lip and as he turned slightly, Strett saw that he wore twin guns on a tooled *buscadero* rig.

He had a notion this was the Count's bouncer or bodyguard, and the man gave the trio a cold going-over before he stepped back behind the curtain. The 'keep returned to his job. Damn Bud Tesser, Strett thought. He's blown things now . . .

'Well, sorry, boys, time for me to be pushing along,' he told the Texan and Rowdy, but they were so involved in pantomiming to their song — and had a large shouting audience now — that they didn't even hear him.

Strett pushed and jostled his way to the side door and stepped out into the cool evening.

Something moved to his right and he spun that way, instinctively lifting an arm to protect his head while his right hand dropped to his gun butt.

But a powerful blow knocked his arm aside and his hat was slammed down on his head at the same time the night exploded in a whirling fireworks display.

But it snuffed out quickly and he felt hands grab him underneath his arms before he passed out all the way.

★ ★ ★

When he came out of it, Strett found himself in a gloomy room that smelled of mouldy wood, damp clothing and general junk. Light filtered in through grimy windows and he had the impression of height: he could hear muted laughter and voices, and footsteps that had the sound of being on a lower floor. Must be in a room on the top floor of the Pleasure Palace, he thought through the throbbing of his skull. He raised his head slowly, just a little, and someone who had been sitting close by moved towards him.

He saw the polished half boots with the shiny Mexican spurs, the dark, whipcord trousers, the *buscadero* gun rig with its matching Colts.

He knew this was the man who had been behind the beaded curtain at the end of the bar. Strett felt fingers twist in his hair and his head was yanked back painfully. He looked up into the narrow face with its thin line of moustache. Bullet-cold eyes bored into him.

Without a word, the man brought his other hand across and smashed it into Strett's face.

Through the ringing in his ears he heard a tired-sounding voice ask, 'Who are you?'

Strett spat blood and managed to get

some on the polished half boots. Two punches rocked him and a knee came up under his jaw. He tumbled into a grey place and from a long way off he heard monotonous cursing. Then, blood streaming from his nostrils, his head was slammed against the wall as the man knelt, gripping him painfully under the jaw, his face inches from Strett's.

'Who — are — you?'

'No one,' Strett slurred. 'Just a drifter looking for a . . . a good time. They told me I'd find it in the Palace — guess they were wrong.'

The back of his skull rapped the timber wall again. 'Why you askin' about the boss?'

'Wasn't — not really. Just talking, was all.'

'Where you get the name French Pete?'

'The Texan told me.'

He winced as the big man rapped him across the bridge of the nose with a gun barrel. '*You* asked *him*!'

Strett's vision was blurred and excruciating agony filled his whole face and head. 'I dunno. Someone said the Count was French. There're a lot of 'French Petes' around.'

'Not many with the name of Lucas — pronounced Loo-car! You know more'n you're saying, mister . . . and you've a look about you. A hunter — you law?'

'Hell, no!' Strett made it emphatic, inferring the last thing he wanted to have anything to do with was the law.

The big man's expression didn't alter. 'Well, if you're right and you've just got a big mouth, you've just dug yourself a grave with it.'

'Judas priest! What is this . . . ? I come in for some pleasure, have a few drinks and a bit of conversation, now you're talking about killing me?'

The man shrugged. 'That depends on the boss, but I'll recommend it to him. He usually takes my advice.'

Strett made himself look worried — and he didn't have to try very hard, either! 'Listen, if I've stumbled into something here, I'm almighty sorry . . . '

'Yeah, you will be.'

Strett ran a tongue around his bleeding lips. 'Christ, man, you're not serious about killing me!'

The big man stood, still holding one of his Colts. He stamped a boot on the floor three times and shortly afterward the door opened. A dark, squat man came in. He was dressed in frock coat, patterned silk-front vest, a shirt with a stiff collar and a blackstring tie, pin-striped trousers and plain cavalry-type half-boots. His face was battered, the nose flattened, and he had a cigar in one hand which he lifted now and drew on it as he walked across to stand beside the big man. He watched Strett with button eyes, rubbing a mangled ear.

'Who is he?' He spoke with a strangled sound.

'Says he's a drifter.'

'You don't believe him?'

'Nah. The French way he said that 'Loo-car' is too much to pass up.'

The Count sighed and nodded. 'I'd like to know how he knows as much as he does before you kill him,' he said and turned away towards the door, drawing comfortably on his cigar.

He was reaching for the handle when Strett said quietly 'Red McKenna.'

The Count stopped dead, his thick shoulders hunched, head thrust forward and wreathed in cigar smoke. Slowly, he turned to look over his shoulder at Strett. His face was the colour of dishwater, his eyes wide and staring.

'Brock's already dead,' Strett told him, and he saw the words strike home like a fist in the teeth.

The bodyguard looked from one to the other, his gun gripped tightly in his fist. Strett saw his own gun now on top of a crate but it was too far for him to risk trying to reach it — at the moment . . .

'Who — did you — say?' The squat man's voice was barely audible.

His thick lips trembled. 'Goddamnit! Answer me!' He was breathing fast and all his words had a choked, gravelly sound.

'Red McKenna — you recollect him, French Pete?'

The Count sagged against the wall near the door, the bodyguard bewildered. Obviously he had never seen his boss shaken so badly before.

'Boss, what the hell . . . ? You all right?'

The man ignored the question, still staring at Strett. 'Who sent you?'

'Red McKenna.'

The Count, or French Pete, made an animal sound, lunged forward, stabbing at Strett's face with his cigar, aiming for an eye.

Then the door burst open and the bodyguard swung around as Cherokee McKenna stepped inside, her Army Colt firing. The ball struck the bodyguard in the left arm, spinning him about. Strett dived past, scooped up his own gun from the crate even as the girl triggered again — but the old percussion cap misfired and there was only a dull *click*!

The bodyguard bared his teeth, brought his gun up and Strett shot him twice in the chest even as the Count tugged a hideaway gun from a vest pocket.

Strett struck out instinctively and the gun barrel broke the Count's wrist and he screamed, twisted away — and crashed through the grimy glass window.

As the glass showered around Strett, the girl got the Colt working again and she fired twice, but by then the squat man's body had disappeared and they heard him scream briefly before he smashed into the street below.

6

The Comanche Way

Strett looked out through the broken glass and the girl shouldered him aside. He could hear her breathing and saw that her nostrils were pinched, outlined in white.

'He moved!' she hissed, raising the smoking gun. 'He is not yet dead!'

Strett forced her hand down and the brown eyes blazed.

'If he's still alive he can talk.'

A slight frown pinched the flesh between her eyes and then she nodded and spun away. He pushed her behind him as two men with drawn guns burst into the room.

'You want to die, buy into this!' Strett snapped, and the men, although lifting their guns, hesitated. Then the second one, the one with the half-breed features and a drooping moustache, bared his teeth and thrust away from his companion, giving Strett two targets.

He nailed them both with two shots so close together they sounded as one, and before the echoes died, he was moving forward, pulling the stunned girl after him by the hand. He kicked a gun out of reach of the nearest man and the half-breed obligingly tossed his weapon out through the open door as he clawed at his bloody side. Strett saw his hand move to a knife close to the wound and kicked him under the jaw.

There was a dim landing and steep narrow stairs that led to the business floor of the Palace. Half-clad women and some trouserless men crowded into doorways, looking at the gunman and the girl in buckskin as they made their way towards the stairs leading down into the lobby and entrance to the bar. A jerk of Strett's gun had them all closing their doors hurriedly.

The girl pulled against him, pointing

to a narrow door at the side. 'Outside stairs,' she said and they hurried towards it.

'What're you doing here anyway?' he asked, jerking open the door. He stepped out with Colt at the ready. It was clear and, as she pushed by, she said, 'I waited an hour for you, then went to see the Count about working here — there was a signal, like someone stamping on the floor above. He ran out, and I followed . . . '

'Just as well you did. I'm obliged.'

By then they had reached the bottom of the stairs and the small crowd that had gathered around French Pete opened out when Strett rudely shouldered through.

'Someone's sent for the sawbones,' a man told them, 'but I don't think he's in town.'

'Sheriff?' snapped Strett, thumbing fresh loads into his Colt as he looked down at the bloody figure at his feet.

'We-ell. A few gunshots and a man fallin' out of a window ain't really enough to bother the sheriff with,' the man told him and Strett grunted, knelt beside French Pete.

The girl was already kneeling, peering closely into his cut and blood-streaked face. It was contorted with pain. Strett figured by the angle of one of the man's legs that it was broken and one arm didn't look too good either. Also there was some bright blood trickling from the whorehouse owner's mouth and Strett wondered if he had busted some ribs and jagged bone had pierced a lung.

'You're a mess, mister,' Strett told him coldly, and the man only stared back, worrying more about his pain than anything else right now.

Until the girl poked him roughly in the side with her gun barrel. He jumped and yelled and the crowd growled and started to press closer. Strett stood, menaced them with his Colt.

'Don't buy into this, gents,' he warned quietly, and some began to back away.

'You are French Pete Lucas?' gritted Cherokee and when he didn't answer she jabbed him in the bloody side again.

After he had yelled, the injured man nodded. 'But — who . . . ?'

'Red McKenna was my father.'

'I — we — never knew he had kids!' He was badly rattled.

'Just me . . . ' She hit him across the face, twice, very hard, and the crowd sucked in a sharp breath, backed-up under the threat of Strett's gun: this didn't concern them and the Count was not a popular man in town, but they were uneasy about it all.

'You're going to die, Lucas!' Cherokee told him calmly, quietly. 'It can be fast or slow. I have lived with Comanches for ten years and I can make you last a week if I have to.'

French Pete's eyes were almost popping from his head. 'I — ' He looked around at the crowd. 'Help me!'

No one moved. One man said,

'Like you helped us citizens when we asked you to try and control the wild-ass trailmen when they shot up the town? You got no help comin', Count, or whatever your name is! My wife wouldn't be in a wheelchair now if you'd clapped a lid on them trail rannies.'

The rest of the crowd seemed in sympathy with the man and the few half-drunk cowboys who had left the Palace to see what was going on, quietly slunk away.

'She wants to know where the others are,' Strett snapped, not happy with the present situation. He figured there must be more men from the Palace who might yet make trouble. He stayed alert despite his own injuries.

French Pete shook his head. 'Dunno . . . I ain't seen any of 'em since . . . '

This time she stood and kicked him in the broken leg. He screamed and passed out.

'That was smart,' Strett said, looking around a little anxiously. 'I think we better be leaving. I saw four men come out the side door of the Palace but I don't know where they are. We make good targets here.'

'But he hasn't talked!'

'It's wait till he does and be in more trouble than we can shake a stick at or . . . '

She dropped to one knee and he heard the knife blade whisper out of her sheath. French Pete came round screaming and the crowd jumped back. She was cutting open the front of the man's trousers.

'You can tell me any time,' Cherokee told French Pete calmly, sawing at the expensive cloth.

'I — I heard the Canuck runs a big spread near Rawlins, Wyoming. I — I swear that's all I know! *Lemme be*!'

'Come on, Cherokee!' Strett said, growing more and more tense as the crowd began to close in again. 'He's scared white — he's likely telling the truth.'

She stared down at the injured man,

face pale and tight, then drew her old Colt and aimed it at his belly.

It was another misfire — and the last straw for the crowd. They couldn't stand for this in their main drag and started to close in, murmuring angrily.

Strett put two shots into the area around at their feet and they scattered. He grabbed the girl and dragged her away although she fought him, tried to get another shot at French Pete, but the old percussion caps either didn't fire or had fallen off the worn nipples.

Then four men came out of the shadows of the Palace and Strett fired into them. They scattered wildly as one man went down sobbing, grabbing at a blood-spurting thigh.

'The horses?' he snapped to the girl, and she pointed across the street. The animals were tethered to a hitch rail outside a barber's shop. She thought ahead, anyway, he allowed.

They sprinted towards them, the crowd scattered now and the Palace men figuring they had seen enough to make them decide to stay out of things eased back into the shadows.

As they sprang into the saddles, Cherokee said, 'The pack horses are behind the livery, all ready to go. I thought we might have to leave in a hurry.'

'Good thinking,' he said, wheeled the bay and ran it down Main, aiming to swing back behind the livery when he reached a dark side street . . .

He was halfway along the block from the Palace when he realized the girl hadn't followed him and, swearing, he slowed, hipped in the saddle.

She had spun her big dun and was spurring it at speed across the street as some of the crowd started back towards French Pete who was struggling to crawl to the boardwalk.

Cherokee McKenna let out what Strett recognized as a Comanche war-cry and the small group of people scattered wildly once more.

French Pete saw her thundering

down upon him, raised a futile arm
an instant before the fast-moving horse
smashed into him.

Strett's mouth tightened as she
wheeled, rode back, cutting loose with
that war-cry once more.

It was the Comanche way, riding a
despised enemy into the ground.

★ ★ ★

She was very quiet on the ride out of
town into the night.

He said nothing to her and she
volunteered nothing. Twice she suddenly
cut away from him and, startled, he
tried to follow the first time. But she
rounded in the saddle, lifted her Colt
threateningly, and, frowning, he waited
by the trail.

When she returned she was pale and
tugged the hat brim down over her
eyes. She took the lead and he had
an idea it was because she didn't want
him to see her face.

The second time she cut away she

didn't return for fifteen minutes and he had been about to go look for her when she showed up.

'All right?' he asked, and it earned him a scathing look but no reply.

Somehow he felt a mite better knowing she was affected by the brutality she had dished out in Wheeler's Falls. She tried hard to hide it but he recognized it for what it was.

At the same time, he had heard stories of Comanche women warriors, but he had never actually seen one. He wondered if she was a member of this very exclusive breed?

They weaved up and down the slopes and he covered their trail as well as he could in the dark. He saw the flickering light of torches once way back through the trees. It might have been a small posse, or a group of men who had worked for French Pete, but they never did catch up with the fugitives.

Strett called a halt by a water-hole

at the beginning of a long valley just before sun-up.

'We'll water the mounts and rest up a spell.'

'No, I — don't need any rest. We keep going.'

It wasn't the best decision but he agreed. He knew adrenalin from the activity in town was still pumping through her — that and perhaps just a little remorse. But it would never be enough to make her turn from the course she had set herself.

Cherokee McKenna didn't care at all about what this vengeance deal might do to her — even if it destroyed her — as long as she killed all five of the men who had murdered her father. That was her only goal in life right now.

He admired her for it, but he felt kind of sad that a young woman as beautiful as she was was on a road to hell.

★ ★ ★

They stayed away from towns, living off the supplies on the pack horses, Strett occasionally shooting a deer. The girl effortlessly trapped small animals with Indian snares and food was never a problem.

Strett avoided the towns, few as they were in this part of Utah and southwest Wyoming, because they would be marked if anyone had notified lawmen to watch for them. A man in the company of a woman in buckskin with identifying deep-chestnut hair, one riding a big bay, the other a grass-fed dun. They could be recognized too easily, especially if anyone had put up a reward.

He didn't think it would happen: it was clear that French Pete — the Count — did not have the respect of the folk of Wheeler's Falls, but maybe there were others who were in the whorehouse with him as a business deal who might wish to bring his killers to heel.

They drifted into wasteland south

of Rock Springs, patchy short grass, pot-holed plains and little water or vegetation. Both were adept at living in the wild but it was still uncomfortable and the nights were bitterly cold even at this time of year. The winds, lazy at any time, slammed down from the north along the chain of the Rockies, buffeted against the Wasatch and were hurled back across this wasteland, with a force that made them tie their hats down.

They huddled under cutbanks, behind hogbacks, amongst boulders, anywhere they might escape the freezing, probing fingers of the wind. No wonder the Shoshone and Arapahoe called it 'Place of the Wayward Winds'.

Then the grass gradually became more prolific and there were patches of scattered, though stunted bush, the odd tree.

From the top of a rise they saw a thin silver ribbon in the distance. Behind it reared the snow-streaked bastion of the Rockies. Strett pointed to the river.

'That ought to be the Yampa. Rawlins is only fifty, sixty miles beyond if it is. But we have a hard climb over the Rockies to get there.'

She shrugged: no obstacle would deter this woman, Strett figured, not on this or any other trail she had to follow to get to the men she wanted to kill.

'This man, the one they call the Canuck — he is a Canadian. Apparently my father never knew his real name . . . '

'He shouldn't be hard to find,' Strett said. 'There aren't that many ranches around Rawlins. Type of country makes it too blamed hard to work cattle, 'specially in winter.'

Cherokee glanced at him sharply. She had been quieter along this trail than when he had first known her, but she had gotten over her long hours of utter silence.

'You seem to have travelled all over.'

'Been here and there.'

'You haven't always been a hired gun-fighter, have you?'

It was his turn to remain silent for a time. He shook his head. 'No, I had a life before I decided to use the gun as a means of making a living — or finding an easy way of dying.'

She frowned. 'You had some great sadness . . . ?'

His mouth tightened a little and briefly she saw the real killer lurking behind that hard-used, wolfish face.

'Yeah — '

She waited.

He said no more.

She wouldn't let it go. 'A woman?'

She recoiled a little at the look in his eyes but then he spoke quietly.

'My wife — my young bride. We had been married only two weeks and I had built a small cabin on a quarter-section I owned along the Neuces River, not far from Corpus Christi. I went across to Laredo to buy a small herd and when I returned . . . ' He paused and looked off into the distance and when he continued his voice was steady, but she could detect an underlying sadness. 'She was dead. Three outlaws had raged through the county while I was gone. They found Jenny alone and unprotected. They used her badly before they finally let her die. The posses that went after the men never found them. But I did. It took me a year to track them all down. One by one. That was when I found out I had a natural man-hunting talent, and a fast draw.'

Her face showed nothing but there was a softness in her eyes. Now she understood why he was helping her — the situations were very similar . . . *he savvied how she felt.*

'Had to wait for the last one to be released from gaol. I called him out in the main drag of the town and beat his draw. A man from Wells, Fargo saw it. He offered me a job, freelance, to trace some stage-coach robbers and I took it. Not caring whether I was successful or if they shot me. It took me a long time to forget how Jenny had looked when I'd found her . . . ' He shrugged and looked at her again. 'I've done a lot of jobs for Wells, Fargo over the years and for anyone else who wanted to hire me. I got over *wanting* to be shot, too.'

'I'm glad you are helping me, Walker Strett,' she said quietly.

After he rolled a cigarette and lit up, he said as he blew out the first lungful of smoke, 'So am I, Cherokee . . . '

They moved on towards the Rockies and the long, hard climb that awaited them.

7

Big Valley Man

Rawlins was a raw frontier town, but there were some signs of 'progress' in the almost completed brick church, which nonetheless had a wooden bell tower, and the neat schoolhouse with its white-painted picket fence.

The business centre was adequate, had the usual percentage of grain and feed stores, a good livery, two saloons, a short street of dubious-looking houses which had a lot of men coming and going at brief intervals, barber's shop, general store and so on. There was a small brick bank with a law office only a few doors away.

It was a town that failed to stir any excitement in Walker Strett — he had seen hundreds like it all over the country. But Cherokee McKenna showed signs of tension and a growing anxiety as they rode slowly down Main. She looked all around her — and earned some stares herself from lounging cowpokes and strolling men. Even those with women at their sides gave her surreptitious looks as she rode towards the livery with Strett.

The hostler barely noticed Strett: his attention was focused fully on the girl.

She met his gaze steadily, unsmiling, and he grunted, turned at last to Strett. He was a big, pale man with a soft look about him, wearing grimy bib-and-brace overalls that were too small. His shirt was grimy, too, and his hair tangled. Naturally enough he smelled strongly of horses.

'Groom and feed the whole outfit,' Strett told him. 'No grain, just oats. We leave our packs here a spell?'

'Sure. No charge. Figurin' on bein' in town for long?'

'A spell,' repeated Strett. 'I hear there's a spread in these parts still hiring before winter.'

The hostler arched heavy eyebrows. 'Where'd you hear that?'

'Couple places. Someone said the rancher's a Canadian.'

The livery man pursed his lips, looking slantwise at the girl now. 'Not around here. Leastways, not that I know of, but then a man in these parts don't necessarily have to say where he's from. Fact, it could be kinda dangerous to ask.'

Strett recognized the clear warning but shrugged casually. 'That's what I was told. I don't care if he's Cross-eyed Pete from Timbuctu, long as he gives me a job.'

'The hell's Timbuctu?'

'Forget it.' Strett flipped the man a silver dollar. 'That cover it for now?'

The man automatically tested the coin between big teeth and nodded. He leaned on his switch broom, watching the girl from behind as she walked back through the doors beside Strett.

The livery man figured they made a dangerous-looking pair.

'Link!' he roared suddenly, looking back down the aisle between the rows of stalls, most of which contained horses. 'Link, you lazy sonuver, git in here!'

A couple of minutes later the outhouse door banged and a gangling youth came hurrying into the big building, jogging awkwardly down the aisle as he tugged up the braces of his overalls.

'I'm here, Pa. Had that bellyache again . . . '

The livery man thrust the switch broom into Link's hands. 'Groom these here broncs and give 'em some oats. Anyone wants me, I'll be at the sheriff's office.'

He made his way via back streets to the rear door of the law building, went in through the cellblock — there were three drunks snoring on the narrow bunks — and into the front office.

Sheriff Nate Cooney looked up, startled, from the book he was writing in, sitting at his scarred old desk. 'The hell you doin' comin' in the back way, Chip?'

'Din' wanna be seen.' The livery man was out of condition and wheezed stale whiskey fumes across the lawman's desk. Cooney reared back. 'Stranger in town — askin' about Mr Sawtell.'

The sheriff looked blank. 'So?'

'He said someone told him he was hirin' hands,' Chip answered irritably. '*This* close to winter? Ain't likely. *An'* he said, he heard he come from Canada.'

'Well, that's s'posed to be where he's from, ain't it? Leastways, that's what you told me.'

'Yeah, that's what Rainey reckons, anyway. But you oughta see this feller, Nate. He's got a look about him. Gunfighter, I reckon. Manhunter. An' he's with a woman dressed in buckskin. She looks Injun to me, mebbe not full-blood, but a good halfway. She's wearin' a gun, too.'

The sheriff had a head slightly too large for his narrow body and his

133

jaw was angular and now thrust out a little.

'Well, no law that says a man can't travel with his squaw.' He stood, a tall man, reached down a high-crowned hat and, after jamming it on the back of his head, took his gunbelt and pistol from a deep desk drawer, the cartridge belt coiled about the holster. 'Best check him out, though. You did right comin' to me, Chip.'

Chip nodded. 'Figured I best let you know — I mean, Mr Sawtell's done plenty for this town an' he did say one time he expected the town to stand between him an' anyone who might bother him. Er — so you'll let him know was me who . . . ?'

'You go back to your livery, Chip. This is for me to handle.' The sheriff spoke curtly and the livery man seemed a mite put out, being dismissed this way.

The couple weren't hard to find in a town the size of Rawlins. Nate Cooney spotted them making for the Rocky

Mountain Café and hurriedly crossed the street, calling, 'Wait up there!'

Strett turned slowly, but the girl snapped her head around sharply. The sun glinted from the star on Cooney's shirtfront and he came up, giving them a half-smile — but not touching his hat brim to Cherokee as he would have if she had been a white woman. 'Sheriff Nate Cooney.'

He waited for their names and Strett gave them somewhat reluctantly. The lawman narrowed his eyes.

'I've heard of you, Strett. You were through here a few years back, before I took over as sheriff. Shot some feller in the saloon.'

'A wanted man, Sheriff. And I was working on a Wells, Fargo warrant.'

'Yeah, still a hired gun.' The lawman's attitude was cooling rapidly. 'What're you doin' here?'

He ignored the girl, but she didn't seem to mind, was maybe used to it.

'Looking for work for the winter.'

'Left your run a mite late, haven't you?'

Strett shrugged. 'Just the way the chips fell . . . between jobs. Nothing in the offing — and I haven't forgotten how to rope or brand a steer.'

Nate Cooney's fingers drummed against the butt of his six-gun. 'Hear you were asking about Mr Sawtell.' As soon as he said the name, the sheriff cursed silently — cursed Chip for not making it clear that Strett hadn't asked for Sawtell by name. Now he'd just identified the rancher for Strett, goddamnit!

'Sawtell? I dunno no Sawtell. I was told there was a ranch still hiring and that the owner came from Canada, that's all.'

Letting me know I've stepped right in it! Cooney thought bitterly. His face was tightening now. 'Well, we don't ask about where a man comes from round these parts. But you won't find no winter work in this district. Take my word for it: someone give you a bum steer. I was you, I'd head on south before the winter comes. It can be mighty long and bitter cold up here if a man ain't got work and — something to keep him warm at night.'

He leered at Cherokee, deliberately insulting. Her face remained impassive.

'Does that make you envious, Sheriff?' she asked and Cooney flushed.

'I ain't no squaw man!' he snapped.

'Just what are you Cooney?' queried Strett tautly. 'Protector of this Sawtell?'

The lawman's face flushed, but his first retort died quickly and, dragging down a deep breath, he said, 'Now why would Mr Sawtell need protectin'?'

'Wouldn't know, but you seem fussed just because I was asking about work with him.'

'Well, I told you he ain't hirin'. *No* one's hirin' round here. So why don't you go try somewheres else?'

'Maybe I will. Thanks for your help, Sheriff.'

Strett signalled Cherokee with his

eyes and they began to walk away from the lawman.

'Hey! Maybe I didn't make myself clear: *There ain't nothin' for you round here!* Only trouble, if you do stick around.'

'I think we savvy that, Sheriff,' Strett replied without turning and he and Cherokee went into the café.

They ate a meal and the waitress was pleasant enough but the big-bosomed woman who ran the place didn't seem too pleased when she saw Cherokee in her buckskins. But she took Strett's money gladly enough, with only a nod by way of 'thank you'.

'I feel better around the tribal campfire than coming into white man's places,' Cherokee commented.

Strett smiled. 'Yeah — I saw how it bothered you.'

She smiled back. 'What now?'

'We make our way up-valley and look over Sawtell's place. Seems he's quite a big man around these parts. Special as far as the townsfolk're concerned.

We might have a hard time getting near him.'

'As long as he's the right man, I don't care about the trouble.'

Chip Westaway, the livery man, greeted them surlily. 'Din' figure you'd be leavin' so soon.'

'Why not?' asked Strett. 'You went to see the sheriff about us, didn't you? He made it clear he doesn't want us around — just because I asked about this rancher Sawtell.'

The big man looked uncomfortable. 'Mr Sawtell's done a heap for this town since he come here a few years back. We kinda look out for him, see he ain't bothered none.'

'What made you think I was going to 'bother' him? I only asked about work.'

'Yeah — but you got it wrong. The Lazy S ain't hired a new hand in more'n two years. Them that work for Sawtell are happy to stay there.'

'Well, no matter. Sheriff told us to move along and that's what we'll do.'

'You sure as hell will!'

The new voice came from the stall next door and both Strett and the girl wheeled as two men appeared. They were obviously cowboys, gun-hung, tough-looking, well fed.

'Lazy S?' Strett asked carefully.

'You bet.' The man who spoke was heavily built with a face that had been on the wrong end of fists most of his life, judging by the scars and twisted nose, slightly lopsided jaw. His big hands were broken-knuckled, too. His name was Dakota and Strett decided he was a brawler.

His companion wasn't as big but he looked plenty tough, wore his gun in a tied-down holster and kept his right hand close to the butt. He went by the name of Cal.

'We'll see you to the county line,' he said in a rumbling voice.

'Reckon we can find it all right,' Strett said, but both men shook their heads slowly.

'Orders.'

'Sheriff or Sawtell?'

'The hell's it matter to you?' snapped Dakota. 'We gonna ride you outa town.'

'No,' Strett said flatly.

The cowboys looked at each other, amused at this.

Chip Westaway ran a tongue over his lips.

'You better do what these gents want,' he told Strett. 'They're Mr Sawtell's bodyguards.'

'Shut up, Chip!' growled the smaller man. He turned to Strett, hand curled around his gun butt tight enough now to make the knuckles white. 'But that was good advice Chip gave you, mister.'

'We'll find our own way . . . ' Strett started to say and then Cherokee said, 'Look out!' She pushed him aside and the gun that the big man had drawn and swung at Strett's head knocked his hat off.

He let himself drop to the straw, rolled, kicked Dakota in the kneecap.

The man howled, danced, fell against the partition, dropping his gun. Cal cursed and started his draw but Strett swept his legs out from under him and the man fell with a thud.

Chip Westaway lunged for a two-pronged hay-fork standing against an aisle post, but Cherokee tripped him, snatched the fork and spun, holding the prongs against the livery man's chest as he lay on the filthy ground.

'No!' she snapped, and Chip wasn't about to give her any argument, not the way she looked.

Meanwhile, Strett had thrown himself onto Cal, grabbed his gun hand and rammed his other arm across the man's throat. Cal lost interest in the gun, released it. All he wanted to do was drag down a good, deep, lung-filling breath. He tried to tear the arm free with both hands.

Strett hit him between the eyes with an elbow and the man slumped, gagging, fighting to stay conscious. Strett grabbed his ears, smashed his head against the stall partition and Cal was out of it.

The big man, still hobbling with his injured knee, tried to swing a kick at Strett's head. The other leg wouldn't support him and he went down awkwardly. Strett brought a knee up into Dakota's battered face, drove him down into a corner. For good measure he kicked him in the side and he fell, groaning.

Strett saw the girl had Chip at her mercy and he wiped sweat from his face, picked up his hat and jammed it on. Breathing a little heavily, he told Cherokee, 'Give him a jab every time he balks at answering.'

She nodded and gave the livery man an experimental touch of the prongs in his chest. He gasped and cringed.

'I dunno nothin'!'

'What's Sawtell got to hide?'

'I dunno — Aaah!' The prongs pierced his overalls front and a little blood stained it in two places. 'Honest! All I know is he — he likes to keep to hisself, don't like anyone askin' about his past. Don't even like folk to thank him for buildin' the church an' the school . . . *Don't*!'

He floundered as the girl jabbed again and Strett gestured at her to hold up.

'He's from Canada?'

The livery man nodded. 'Yeah, yeah, everyone knows that . . . '

'How old is he?' Cherokee snapped and Chip blinked.

'Hell, I dunno. Older'n me. Got some grey in his hair.'

Her face was grimly triumphant as she looked at Strett.

'Not much to go on, Cherokee.'

'Enough for me! He is from Canada, about the right age and — *he has something to hide*!'

'You wouldn't want to make a mistake.'

Dakota started to come round and crawled towards his gun lying half buried in the straw. Strett stomped brutally on his hand and the man howled, hugged the hand against his chest. Strett scooped up the six-gun, swept the weapon in a short arc and knocked Dakota cold. Cal was moaning but no threat.

Chip had never been a threat and he cowered now as Strett turned to him.

'I dunno nothin' else, I swear!'

Strett ignored him. 'C'mon, Cherokee. We better go.'

She agreed and they made Westaway saddle their mounts and help load the pack horses. They cleared town by back streets, headed for the hills, but once in the cover of the trees, they swung back and, sticking to heavy timber, they made their way up-valley in the direction of Sawtell's Lazy S ranch.

★ ★ ★

The man who called himself Miles Sawtell was swarthy and his darkness was made more noticeable by the beard that was shot through with grey. His short hair was speckled with silver and his face was long and narrow, weathered by many seasons. The eyes were hard and brittle.

Dakota, his hand bandaged, told him what had happened at the livery in Rawlins. Sawtell swore angrily.

'You goddamn fools! If ever there was a way to make this stranger suspicious, you two picked it!'

'His name's Walker Strett, boss,' Dakota said, nursing his hand and favouring his left leg, the one with the damaged kneecap, vainly hoping for some sign of sympathy from the rancher. 'Nate Cooney says he's a hired gun.'

Sawtell went very still. 'The question being *who* hired him . . . that fool Cooney put him on to me, no doubt!'

'Strett said someone told him you was hirin' for winter and that you come from Canada . . . '

'That was his excuse for asking about me, you dumb son of a bitch! Christ, I pay you enough! Why the hell can't you at least *try* to earn it!'

'Boss,' Cal said in a hurt voice, 'that's what we figured we *was* doin'. Aimed to ride him an' his squaw across the county line after Cooney come into the bar an' told us what was goin' on. We figured that's what you'd want.'

The rancher sighed, nodding, made a cutting gesture with his hand. 'Yes, yes, I guess you tried your best. But, dammit! You've only made this Strett more suspicious! Why's he dragging a squaw around with him, anyway doesn't sound like any gunfighter that I've ever heard of?' He paused, frowning. 'Where are they now?'

He knew by their sheepish look that they had lost track of them and he threw up his arms. 'Judas priest! Take some men and look around!'

'Yeah, boss, we'll find 'em,' Dakota assured him quickly. 'You stay put just in case they are after you.'

Sawtell's face tightened, his mouth no more than a razor-slash now.

'If they are, *you keep them away*

from me! Kill them if there's no other way. Now get!'

The two crestfallen hardcases hurried out, both moving awkwardly so as to favour their injuries.

Sawtell went to his gun cupboard and unlocked the mahogany doors, swinging them open. He stared in at the large array of pistols and high-powered rifles, trying to decide which ones he ought to start packing with him wherever he went from now on.

Until this Strett and the mystery Indian girl either made their intentions clear . . .

Or were dead.

8

Little War

They weren't prepared for the size of the Lazy S.

Strett and Cherokee found their way into high country that overlooked the north-east end of the long valley and on the way they had passed a cross-roads sign burned in weathered timber, pointing to 'Sawtell's' and another ranch, 'Rainey's'.

Now, from the high country, they could see that the ranch took up the entire end of this part of the valley and, apparently, overflowed into the hills and flats beyond.

'He's gonna have one helluva big crew working a place like that,' Strett allowed, lowering his field-glasses, passing them to the girl.

But she didn't raise them to her eyes:

even anyone with poor sight could see how immense the Lazy S was.

'Perhaps it will be harder than we thought to get close to this Sawtell,' she said musingly, 'but we will do it.' She looked squarely at Strett. 'We *must* do it! I must confront him. I wish him to know why I am killing him.'

He nodded slowly. 'Let's make sure he's the one you want first.'

'He is the man, Strett! I sense it!'

He shrugged. She was likely right, but . . . ah, he was probably being too fussy. It was just that he had always operated that way: made absolutely certain of his facts before moving against a man. Even when he *knew* his quarry to be a dyed-in-the-wool outlaw, he made certain-sure the man *had* been involved in the particular crime he was chasing him for.

Now he glanced up at the sky. 'Be sundown soon. We'd best find a camping place and we can look around better tomorrow.'

She agreed and they climbed the slope until they came to a small waterfall with a grass-and-brush bench to one side. An ideal spot.

They kept the camp-fire small, taking normal precautions in dangerous country. The cold closed in early and they both wished they could have built up the fire for warmth. But Cherokee finally scraped out a pit, burned some deadwood in it, shielding the small blaze with rocks and cut brush. Strett knew what she was doing and after some hesitation approved, and got his own shallow trench going. They managed to contain the light from the blaze but there was nothing they could do about the smoke. It might be too dark to be seen, but there was the pungent smell of the wood . . . drifting down the slope with the chill night wind.

They scraped thin layers of earth over the still glowing embers and laid first green branches, then their bedrolls on top. In minutes they were snug and warm, and sleep was induced quickly.

Strett figured to take one last look around but the warmth seduced him and he drifted into early sleep.

He awoke to a savage kick in the side that lifted him half out of his bedroll. Hurting, his instincts still took over, and he rolled away from the direction of the kick, snatching the six-gun he had taken into his bedroll with him. But someone was waiting and a knobbly stick crashed down across his forearm, the gun tumbling away. As he spun towards the attacker, arm throbbing painfully, the stick slammed him across the side of the head in a backhand blow.

He went down and out, the echo of the girl's angry tirade in Comanche drifting into the edge of the blackness that enfolded him . . .

★ ★ ★

Voices slowly penetrated the crashing pain that filled his head and he had the metallic taste of old blood in his mouth.

' . . . tried to cover their tracks,' a rumbling voice that he vaguely recognized was saying, 'but once we picked 'em up just below the high trail, we figured they'd take the easy campsite up by the falls. An' there they was, sleepin' like babes.'

'You should've kept them there and sent for me instead of bringing them down here!' griped another voice.

There was a sigh and a second voice that Strett recognized said, 'Boss, we figured we'd have a better chance of holdin' 'em here and doin' whatever you want than out in them hills . . . '

'But I don't want any trouble on this place, goddamnit! I don't need attention — 'specially from the law!'

Another weary sigh. 'OK, but this one ain't law.'

'Hey, he's coming to!'

Rough hands grabbed Strett, hauled him to a sitting position and slammed him back violently against a plank wall.

He could smell hay and old grease and rusted iron and damp wood. *Barn*, he thought before he got his eyes open far enough to confirm it.

He recognized Dakota and Cal and there was another man with them, tall, swarthy, well dressed. It had to be Sawtell. The man leaned down closer in the dim light inside the barn from the reflected watery sun. It hurt to turn his neck, but Strett did so, looking for the girl.

She was lying on some straw, bound hand and foot and gagged. He even managed a half-smile, remembering the way she was cussing-out the attackers just before he passed out.

'So you're Walker Strett,' said Sawtell and, when he said nothing, Cal nudged him roughly with a boot toe.

'Mr Sawtell's talking to you!'

Strett raised his eyes, every fibre of his being seemingly on fire. He nodded very gently, but his brain still seemed to flop around inside his skull.

'Gunfighter, bounty hunter, hired

gun. So what the hell're you doing giving me a pain in the butt?'

'Only asked about a job,' Strett said, making himself gasp, sitting limply and wincing occasionally. He felt like hell, but it wouldn't hurt for these men to get the notion he was a lot worse than he actually was.

'You lie!' snapped Dakota and kicked Strett's leg hard.

'Take it . . . easy, dammit!' breathed Strett, looking up at the rancher. 'I was in Fort Collins and a feller I met in a bar told me I might find winter work near Rawlins. 'A Canuck named Sawtell', he said. That's what brought me here . . . so lay off the rough stuff, goddamn you!' he finished, as Dakota kicked his leg again.

'What was this feller's name?' demanded Sawtell.

Strett shook his head. 'Smitty — Paddy . . . I dunno. We'd bought each other quite a few drinks by that time.'

'Can't recollect his name, only mine!'

'You were more important to me! I needed — *still* need — a job to see me through the winter!'

'So you brought your squaw along? What you think she was gonna do? Crawl into your bunk each night to keep you warm? With the others looking on?'

'She's not my *squaw*. We met along the trail. She got me out of a little trouble and she was comin' north to see some kinfolk on the Pathfinder Reservation, and Rawlins happens to be on the way.'

'He's lyin', boss!' growled Dakota, nursing his bandaged hand, eyes glittering. 'Lemme work him over a little.'

Sawtell lifted a cautioning finger, watching Strett. 'A man like you ought to be able to find better work for the winter than riding line on a Wyoming spread.'

Strett squirmed. 'Well, it might be uncomfortable and don't pay much but . . . it'd actually be a mite healthier for

156

me . . . up there in the snow country where kinfolk of a certain recently dead outlaw won't think of looking for me.'

Sawtell almost smiled. 'Bit off more than you can chew for once, huh?'

'It happens once in a while.'

'Boss, Cooney din' believe him either,' Cal said, 'and they scared Chip Westaway white. But he said the squaw was definitely askin' after you and she thought you were the man she wanted.'

Sawtell thought about that, walked over to a work bench, picked up a file and idly checked the point. He turned, leaning his hips against the bench. 'Untie her and take off the gag.'

'She'll bad-mouth you for sure . . . ' warned Cal.

'Do it!'

The girl merely glared hotly and rubbed her raw wrists after she was free. She tried to stand but her legs were numbed from being so long tied up. She crawled across to Strett.

'You are all right? Your head is swollen and cut.'

'I'm OK. They hurt you?'

She shook her head. 'Not yet.'

'Ah, expecting to be given rough treatment, are you?' Sawtell said, stepped forward suddenly, twisted his fingers in her chestnut hair and flung her backwards. 'Just who the hell are you?'

Strett saw what she was going to do and shook his head warningly, but it hurt too much and he grimaced, held his head in both bands, tried to call to her. 'Don't say it!'

But she sat up, leaning back on her arms, glowering at Sawtell. 'I am the daughter of the man you murdered eleven years ago!

Sawtell started, stepped back, squinting down at her. 'Who?' he asked tautly.

'Red McKenna!'

The rancher frowned more deeply and then released a breath he hadn't been aware of holding, shook his head. He was tight about the lips and his

158

nostrils were edged with white. 'I — I don't know any Red McKenna!'

'You lie! You and the others killed him! I *watched* from the cabin! You trapped him in the river and — '

'Get the bitch out of here!' Sawtell snapped suddenly to Dakota and Cal. 'I'm not in the mood for this. Get rid of them both.'

Dakota, turning from the struggling girl, leaving her to Cal, looked sharply at Sawtell. 'Just how you want to get rid of 'em, boss?'

'Judas priest, Dakota! What the hell d'you think I mean? *Get rid of them!* Rainey's probably behind this. Send 'em back to him, any way you like. Just, for Chris'sakes, get it done!'

Dakota flinched some at the man's tone and nodded, grabbed Strett's shirt and heaved him to his feet. The gunfighter swayed drunkenly, the barn spinning around him. Cal had the girl's arms pinioned now, was fumbling to get lengths of rawhide wrapped around her wrists.

Strett stopped in front of Sawtell. 'I don't know anyone named Rainey . . . I just wanted a job . . . '

Sawtell hit him hard in the midriff. Strett gagged, doubled-up, and Sawtell bared his teeth and lifted a knee into his face. As the man dropped to his knees, gasping, the rancher twisted his fingers in Strett's hair, yanked his head back and spat in his face.

'Now get outa my life, you son of a bitch! You bit off more'n you can chew this time!' The man was incensed. 'I've had a bellyful of Rainey! Send a hired gun after me, huh?' He swore bitterly and then kicked Strett in the chest and the man fell unconscious. Dakota lifted him without much effort, although he favoured his injured hand, started to drag him to a corner where Strett's big bay waited beside the girl's dun.

'See that it looks like an accident!' Sawtell snapped and strode out into the watery sunlight, heading back towards the house. 'I've already drawn too much attention.'

Cal had the girl's hands tied and he lifted her into the saddle of the dun. 'Hey, Dak,' he said in a hoarse whisper, 'are we s'posed to kill 'em or just beat the tar outa them?'

'I ain't too sure, but — you know the way he acts. We better kill 'em. But first, we have some fun with that li'l beauty!'

He pursed his lips and made smacking sounds in the girl's direction. Her eyes were murderous and although she never spoke, Dakota was aware of a prickling feeling on the back of his neck . . .

They took them into the foothills and followed a creek into a heavy stand of timber, the hanging willows making deep shadows on the water and the cattails.

'Just round the bend is that old stone cabin,' Dakota said. 'We'll do it there, dump the bodies down one of them bottomless canyons back in the hills.'

Strett had been draped across his horse, arms dangling limply one side,

161

legs the other. He had been conscious for the last mile or so, but had refrained from making a sound. Through the roaring in his ears, he heard Dakota's words, swivelled his eyes and managed to glimpse the girl tied to her big dun.

Then they started to ford the creek, the horses' hooves clunking on the stones underfoot. The water level rose halfway up Strett's legs and it was icy and he just managed to stifle his gasp in time.

Then, as Cal's horse stumbled and splashed wildly, whinnying, Dakota trying to haul his own mount aside, Strett let himself slide silently off the bay into the water. He went straight to the bottom, reached down and grabbed a slippery rounded rock larger than his fist.

As he surged back to the surface, he heard Dakota yelling, the man reaching for his gun. Strett kept thrusting with his aching leg muscles, launched himself bodily at the man, smashing the rock into the middle of his face.

Cal shouted, still trying to right his horse, snatched at his gun, as the two bodies tumbled back into the water. It was all bloody about Dakota's head and Cal took time to stare, and then Strett got his footing and his right hand came boiling out of the creek holding Dakota's six-gun.

He triggered three times and Cal was blasted back over the rump of his prancing horse. He plummetted into the water which was shallower there and then Strett grabbed his bay's reins with his free hand, swung the smoking, streaming gun around to Dakota.

But the big man was floating face-down in a patch of reddish water . . .

Cherokee McKenna stared at him with her big eyes.

Strett fought to stay on his feet, his own head wound bleeding again now. He gave her a somewhat shaky look.

'Reckon we'd best get outa here.'

He released her and they left the dead men but took their guns and spare ammunition and the two of them rode into the hills.

'We're not quitting this valley!' she told him curtly.

He looked resigned as he replied, 'Didn't figure we were . . . '

But they had ridden only another 400 yards when three men with rifles appeared on the trail before them, the one in the middle wearing wire-framed spectacles.

As they hauled rein, he gestured down towards the creek. 'Them two've needed killing for a long time. Like your moves, mister, whoever you are. Me, I'm Tim Rainey, and I'd like to have a talk with you . . . '

Strett figured there wasn't much choice about that as the rifle barrels continued to menace both himself and the girl.

★ ★ ★

Rainey's place wasn't even one-third the size of Sawtell's Lazy S. But it was well-enough run, judging by the condition of the buildings and the layout of the ranch. The horses in the corrals looked to be in good condition, as did the cattle they passed on the way in.

Rainey took them into the ranch house, all guns sheathed by now, and sat them down in an austerely furnished parlour whose timber walls were a fine mellow colour from many seasons of smoke from the big fireplace. It was a man's house and he called an Indian woman from the kitchen and told her to bring coffee.

Rainey leaned back in his chair, pressed his fingertips together and squinted at Strett and Cherokee over the tops of his glasses. He blinked and lifted his spectacles, rubbing gently at his eyes.

'So, it's Walker Strett and Cherokee. And what've you done to upset Sawtell?'

Before answering, Strett glanced out the window and saw the lantern-jawed foreman Rainey had called Mesquite lounging against a porch post, smoking, arms folded, waiting patiently — for something.

Rainey saw the direction of his gaze and smiled thinly. He was a pinch-faced man, a little stoop-shouldered, but there was a stoniness about his eyes that made Strett wary of the man. It wouldn't surprise him to learn that Rainey had once been a lawman. The only other choice was that of cold-blooded killer, but somehow this rancher didn't quite come across as being that dangerous. But he seemed to be a hard man in his own right, judging by the way his men jumped when he gave an order — and only once, too: on the ride in he'd never had to repeat himself.

'What's your interest in this?' Strett asked quietly.

Rainey spread surprisingly big, work-hardened hands. 'Me and Sawtell don't get along. He's got three times as much land as me, but he wants half my water. We've tangled on and off over the year. Couple of men on both sides have — well, kinda moved on.'

'Or *been* moved on,' opined Strett, and Rainey smiled faintly, shrugged.

'Been the odd angry shot traded as well. He wants to take over part of the river that cuts across my land. But I've got legal title. He don't need any more water, anyway. It's just an excuse to try to squeeze me out. There's been a lot of investigatin' by both sides and my man happened to come across somethin' that Sawtell was hidin'.'

He glanced at Cherokee as she leaned forward, elbows on her knees, face tight with interest. Rainey frowned slightly.

'Seems there's a hint, just talk really, 'cause if I could really prove anythin' I damn well would — but the general gist is Sawtell come down from Canada years ago and they say he was on the drift, the seat outa his pants, a grub-liner. Then one day he's suddenly rich, throwing money round like a whole bunch of drunken cowhands. Came north, bought up half this valley. Tried to buy me out, too, but I weren't interested in sellin'. Stayed friendly for a spell but then he started this river deal.'

The girl was showing a lot of interest by now. Strett rolled a cigarette with stiff fingers. 'You never found out how he suddenly became rich?'

Rainey shook his head. 'Just a rumour or two started by some feller who seemed to know him . . . but he rode on one night and no one ever saw him again.'

'Rode on, or disappeared?' asked Strett quietly.

'We-ell, he claimed Sawtell used to run with a wild bunch down in Arizona and they pulled a big job, busted up and went their own ways.'

'You seem to have dug deeply into Sawtell's past,' Cherokee said. 'I just wonder how deep — '

'How deep you want, li'l lady?'

'Do you know the names of any of

the men Sawtell was supposed to have ridden with?'

'Only a couple, but I know that the wild bunch called themselves the Werewolves — You all right, miss?'

Cherokee sucked in a sharp breath as she looked quickly at Strett. 'My father used to tell me stories about a band of men calling themselves the Werewolves! They were good men, led by someone calling himself Red Wolf. They fought the lawless, helped the poor.'

Rainey's laughter burst through the room and he held up a hand, still amused, as Cherokee shot him a murderous glare.

'Cherokee, you gotta forgive me! See, I know about this wild bunch. I was an Arizona lawman for a spell and twice I was in posses chasin' 'em. And take it from me they was no do-gooders. They musta held up twenty stages that I know of, trains with express cars, banks. They shot their way out when they had to. Your daddy surely got his trails crossed if he figured the Werewolves were good fellers!'

She was still angry. 'I know they weren't *true* stories! Just ones he made up to amuse me . . . I knew that even when I was a child . . . but I often wondered if Red Wolf was meant to be him. He made him the hero of all the stories.' She turned towards Strett. 'Could it be so that if I ever learned he *had* ridden with the real Werewolves, that I might not think so badly of him?'

Strett spoke quietly. 'Cherokee, I've worked a good deal for Wells, Fargo and like Rainey said, that Werewolf bunch hit plenty of stages and express cars. Very smart and mean. Managed to slip the law for years. Then they suddenly stopped operating. The word was that they'd broken up, a few even claimed some members were caught for minor crimes and jailed. But this is the first I knew that your father might've been one of the Werewolves.'

'I know my father was never in

prison. And, until now, I thought the Werewolves was just a made-up name.'

Strett said nothing, but Rainey frowned, looking from one to the other. 'Am I missin' somethin' here?'

Strett glanced towards the girl, but she seemed engrossed in her own thoughts now. His gaze was steady on Rainey's pinched face.

'Cherokee's father was killed by five men. She doesn't know why, but, in the light of what you've just said and she's told us, he could've ridden with them and they had a grudge against him, tracked him down and evened the score. She knew he was some kind of outlaw before he went straight.'

Rainey was frowning now, his eyes pinched down behind the lenses, tensed. 'What was your father's name?'

'Red McKenna.'

Rainey's expression didn't change, but he pursed his lips, then slowly shook his head. 'No, can't say I ever heard of anyone named McKenna bein' one of the Werewolves, but we did have some names . . . Brock, a Negro name of Burns, feller called Idaho — he drowned in '74 — and a feller callin' himself French Pete.'

He broke off at the way Cherokee and Strett both jerked their heads up. 'I say somethin'?'

'French Pete was the one who put us on to Sawtell,' Strett said slowly, adding a brief outline of the incidents in Wheeler's Falls. 'Pete — or the Count as he called himself didn't actually name Sawtell. Called him the Canuck, said he had a spread outside of Rawlins. Cherokee knew that one of the men who murdered her father was called the Canuck.'

Tim Rainey sighed and leaned back in his chair. 'Yeah, I heard about that Count feller and his bodyguard bein' killed. You two, huh?' He gave the girl a hard look, shook his head. 'Well, I've seen some hard things in my time, but damned if I'd've ever picked Miss Buckskin here for that kind of chore.'

'My father was a good man, whatever

you think,' the girl said curtly. 'I loved him and I *will* find his murderers.'

Rainey nodded. 'So, you're after revenge. And you, Strett? You're just helpin' out, right?'

Strett shrugged and Rainey smiled thinly.

'You two could be useful to me.'

'Yes,' Cherokee said slowly. 'Do your dirty work.'

Rainey laughed. 'Got some smart behind them big brown eyes, ain't you, li'l lady?' He glanced at Strett whose face was stony, eyes as unreadable as ancient Greek to Rainey.

'Look, we can all scratch each other's back here — Cherokee gets to nail one of the men who killed her daddy, and you, Strett — well, I guess just helpin' her would bring its own rewards, huh?'

He laughed at the expression on Strett's face. 'No use you lookin' that way, Strett, I'm holdin' all the aces. So what'll it be? Help me with my little war with Sawtell, or do I get myself in real good with him by takin' you both back, all tied-up like hogs headed for the slaughterhouse?'

At some unseen signal, Mesquite entered quietly from the porch, gun drawn, the hammer cocked.

9

Squared Away

The herd was in the first of a series of canyons on the south-western side of the valley. It was a large herd, but because of the way the canyons lay and could only be reached by twisting trails, there was only a small group of riders in charge.

There was an old chuckwagon near a cooking fire, rolled soogans scattered about amongst the saddles and work gear. The cook, favouring one leg, scrubbed away at burnt pots and two men appeared to be sleeping in their bedrolls, likely the ones due for nighthawk later.

From the rim of the canyon, Strett studied the camp and then eased back to where Cherokee sat, idly stripping a long blade of grass. The sun was westering and it laid a cold look across the sky, a mixture of lavender and pink. Strett buttoned his jacket as he squatted beside the girl who seemed comfortable enough in her usual buckskins, twisting the grass into twine.

'Six riders and a cook. Couple of hundred cows, could be more in one of the canyon off-shoots.'

She glanced up, measuring the twine against a shaped stick that already had a bow's curve in it, but could be drawn into a stronger one with the cord she was making. 'You don't like what Rainey wants us to do, do you?'

'Still got some cattleman in me, I guess. Never did care to destroy good beef, even in the war when it meant starving out the enemy.'

'I like the idea.' But she didn't look at him as she set down the bow stick and made more twine.

'That don't surprise me.'

'Why not?' Her eyes blazed. 'Sawtell helped murder my father, *and* he was going to have his men kill us.'

'Yeah — well, we do what Rainey wants, or we're in trouble. Not much of a choice.'

'You let him bully you into it. I was surprised.'

He shrugged. 'Saw it as a way for you to reach Sawtell. No way we could get close to him with all those men he has. This way, it makes him mad and he comes after us.'

She stood suddenly, once again measuring her cord against the bow, took her knife and began cutting notches in the tapered ends. 'That is all I am interested in — reaching Sawtell. *How* we do it does not matter.' She glanced at him. 'Then we can move on to the next murderer.'

'Have to find out where he is first.'

'Rainey said he will tell me a clue — *after* Sawtell is finished.'

'Yeah, while Rainey sits pretty. We're gonna have to clear this neck of the woods in a hurry. Rainey's setting us up to take the blame for whatever happens to Sawtell. Rainey's the one gonna come outa this best of all. Sawtell won't be a problem for him any more and, far as Sheriff Cooney and the rest of Rawlins are concerned, we'll be the ones to come after.'

She shrugged. 'It doesn't matter, as long as I find out where to look for the next man.'

'There'll only be one more after Sawtell — if what Rainey says about Idaho Reese drowning is true.'

Her glance was sharp. 'Why would he make up something like that?'

'No idea. Just wondering how he knows. But, if he's an ex-lawman like he says, I guess he's picked it up on the grapevine.'

She gave him one of her puzzled, half-exasperated looks at the expression but he did not explain. Instead he nodded at the bow as she started to make a loop in the cord to fit into the notch. 'Looks pretty good.'

'Yes, I make good bows. Some warriors used to pay me to make bows for them. It will be ready for tonight . . . '

★ ★ ★

The moon was covered by scudding clouds at random intervals and they waited until a large, anvil-shaped cloud moved across the moon's face before riding into the canyon.

The nighthawks were lazy types, stopping for a yarn and a smoke whenever they met on their slow circuit of the herd. Not that the cows were giving any trouble: this was a well-grassed holding canyon and they all had full bellies. All of which made it easier for Strett and Cherokee to move into position behind and slightly above the camp where four men tossed and snored in their bedrolls. The fire had been banked to provide hot coffee for the nighthawks and it was easy for Strett to walk in, hide the saddles in a deep crevice, then drop a handful of percussion caps into the fire.

179

By the time he had gone back past the last sleeper, the caps were starting to explode with sharp, vicious little cracks, the copper casings flying with stinging force through the camp. The cowboys jerked awake, not knowing what was happening — it didn't sound like an attack because the noise wasn't like gunfire. The coffee pot tipped over though and sizzled and hissed and embers flew wildly, some landing on their blankets. Thick white smoke-clouds filled the camps choking, blinding. While they were yelling and stamping and looking around bewilderedly, Cherokee moved in on the sleeping herd, struck a match and shielded its flame with her slim body while she applied it to the tuft of dry grass and twigs tied to the end of the blunt arrow shaft she had fitted to the small bow she had made that afternoon.

She had weighted the arrow's nose with a stone and it arced up and over the now disturbed cattle, landed accurately in the midst of a knee-high patch of grass. Sparks showered and although she had a second arrow ready, she saw she would not need it.

The herd was already up, bellowing and stomping, wheeling this way and that — the fire amongst them, the crackle of the percussion caps behind. The only way to go was out through the narrow, twisting entrance, and with one accord they made their rush. The nighthawks frantically got out of the way.

By now the cowboys knew what was happening, some shooting wildly into the night, the din only adding to the herd's panic. They wheeled so tightly they weren't in line with the narrow opening to the exit, but on an angle with the camp where the cowboys were now tugging on boots and looking for the saddles which Strett had quietly removed earlier. Panic was now spreading amongst them when they realized they were afoot.

Someone heard the rumble of hoofs

and the approaching bawling and then there were startled yells from the cowhands as they started to run. The cook fell, got up and limped madly away, cannoning into a cowboy. None of the others had both their boots on, one man had only his stockinged feet. They clambered wildly into rocks, the cook struggling to get his bulk up into the low branches of a tree.

Then, the herd charged through the camp and pots and pans clanged and dented and frightened the cattle even more. The chuckwagon tilted, finally fell, was trampled to splinters underfoot. The cowhands started shooting in an effort to drive the cattle away from them. The nighthawks were the only ones mounted, as soon as they had seen the stampede start, they had run for the back of the canyon where the walls sloped before becoming sheer. Now they were well out of range and could do nothing when Cherokee and Strett came riding in, screaming Comanche war-whoops, firing into the milling steers, turning them towards the exit.

The terrified beasts lunged and plunged, balked and bawled, but the inevitable press pushed them into the narrow passage of the exit. Some went down and the pile-up began.

But those behind pushed so relentlessly that the front of the mob rode up and over the thrashing downed steers, spilled into the high-walled passage, driven on by the terror of gunfire and wild yells behind.

The cowboys were shooting at the raiders now, but with the nighthawks adding their guns to the racket, their bullets crossed and they were soon ducking their own pards' flying lead.

Strett and Cherokee charged after the herd that was now pounding along the twisting trail out of the canyon. They emptied their hot guns, reloaded on the run, started shooting again, hazing the herd on and on . . .

At the sharp bends, there were casualties, but the rest were moving so fast and determinedly that they merely trampled their companions into the dust and kept on.

All at once they were clear of the canyon trail and heading across the valley, starting to scatter. Strett charged his sweating, snorting bay through the still-bunched sections, breaking them up. The girl saw what he was doing, had no choice but to follow suit. In minutes, the survivors of the stampede had been scattered to hell and gone across the valley and into some of the low, brush-choked hills beyond. None of the steers would stop running before morning unless it was from sheer exhaustion. It would take weeks for Sawtell's men to gather them again.

Sweating, panting, Strett met Cherokee as she hauled rein by a clump of rocks. Even in the dim light he could make out her critical look.

'You did not do as Rainey wanted!' she accused. 'They were supposed to run over the bench and down into that shattered country with all the holes and ditches where they would break their legs . . . '

'And die a lingering death,' he said curtly. 'No point in letting them die that way. They're still out of Sawtell's reach for weeks. You've got too much Comanche in you.'

'I think Rainey will not be pleased,' she said sharply.

'How about you, Cherokee?' he asked stiffly.

She looked at him coolly for a long moment — then wheeled her mount and rode away. He followed, letting the sweating bay make its own pace.

★ ★ ★

The men were red-eyed come sun-up and the cattle were still scattered to hell and gone. Bighorn, the top-hand who had been in charge of the canyon herd, looked pale and drawn, as if just returned from cutting loose the wolf in town for a week.

He cussed and snapped at his men

185

and all the time kept looking towards the trail leading out from the ranch house. He'd sent a man with the news. When he saw the roil of dust, his belly tightened and he gritted his teeth and went to the trail where it entered the canyon to await Sawtell.

Trouble was, he knew he was going to be blamed for this . . . which made him glad that Dakota and Cal were dead. If they'd been around Sawtell would have turned them loose on him. Still, he kept other hardcases on the payroll . . .

Sawtell was forking his big chestnut gelding with the white dollar-sized blaze above the left eye. Bighorn didn't even take note of who was riding with him, just watched and swallowed nervously as the rancher rode up. Sawtell lashed his quirt across the cowboy's face, almost spilling him from the saddle.

'You son of a bitch! You were warned to keep your goddamn eyes open!'

Bighorn rubbed at the stinging welt

that ran from his left ear across his cheek, just beneath his eye. His nose had been cut deeply and blood trickled down his face.

'Boss, we never figured anyone'd come that deep into the canyons . . . '

'You never figured!' Sawtell mocked, fuming. Bighorn flinched as the man lifted his quirt again, but changed his mind. 'Aaah — where the hell are my cows? I don't see more'n twenty in sight.'

The cowhand swallowed, noting now that Sawtell had brought two of his hardcases, Mitch Badell and Howie Case. Their brutish faces were blank, big hands folded on saddlehorns, awaiting orders.

'They're scattered way back into the foothills, boss, I got the boys roundin'-up.'

'It'll take weeks! I'll miss the best market in Cheyenne, you blamed idiot.' Sawtell turned to the hardcases. 'See this incompetent bastard off Lazy S.'

'Like hell!' snapped Bighorn, lifting

his reins and wheeling his mount. He rammed hard into Sawtell's chestnut and the horse went down, shrilling, the rancher rocking in the saddle, finally falling free.

Bighorn spun back as Badell and Case closed in, lifted his coiled rope from the horn and caught Case across the jaw. The man rocked wildly — right into the path of Badell's horse. There was a wild mêlée and by then Bighorn's mount was running for the hills . . .

Gunshots crashed behind him and he lay along his mount's back, but the bullets fell short. He looked towards the hills, back at the mess of men and horses.

By God! He was going to make it safely!

* * *

And he did. That is, he reached the first of the foothills, rammed his mount into the brush and timber and weaved away from the open country. Once he looked back and glimpsed through the branches the three riders coming at a gallop. Sawtell waved an arm, spreading out the hardcases, himself coming in almost in line with Bighorn.

He spurred his weary horse forward — it had been involved in trying to stop the stampede last night and then the widespread hunt for cows that morning — and up the slope, gaining ground as he hauled rein to the right and hit a level section. He rode fast for ten minutes, taking the lashing of low branches across his already bloody face, losing some skin, his clothes tearing.

He stopped and listened and above the pounding of his heart and the blowing of his horse, he heard the pursuers — and they were below him! Obviously didn't know he had come this high!

Bighorn grinned and straightened, starting to yank around the reins. Then he froze.

A man and a girl in buckskin sat their mounts across his trail beside a clump of rocks. Both held rifles trained on him and he noticed the small bow hanging on the girl's saddlehorn. He knew at once who they were and felt the blood drain out of his face as he lifted his hands slowly.

'I ain't lookin' for trouble!'

'No, you're running from it by the looks of things,' said Strett. 'You in that camp last night?'

Bighorn nodded, mouth tightening some. 'Yeah — you sure gave us hell.'

'Where is Sawtell?' snapped the girl impatiently.

Bighorn gestured below with his head. 'Him and two hardcases. They catch me they'll likely kill me now.'

'Call out,' ordered Strett.

Bighorn blinked. 'Wha-at?'

'Let out a yell like your horse has slipped or something.'

'You're loco! I do that and — '

Bighorn let out a wild yell involuntarily as Cherokee jumped her mount forward, ramming it into the cowboy's horse.

Bighorn threw himself from the saddle as his horse's hoofs broke away the edge of the trail and it lost balance, slid on its haunches and then rolled on to its back, sliding and kicking and whinnying all the way down the slope, engulfed in a cloud of dust.

Bighorn sprawled, looking up wild-eyed at the others. Strett jerked his rifle.

'Just stay put. Make like you're hurt.'

'Or we can really hurt you to make it look good,' the girl said in casual menace, and Bighorn stayed put, wondering if he could get a hand on to his six-gun.

Strett and the girl moved back into the rocks, but Bighorn knew he was still under their rifles. Downslope, he heard men yelling, then the effort of horses heaving up the hillside towards him. His fingers dug into the gravel. His breathing was fast. His heart hammered. He was getting ready to heave up and take his chances when a gun crashed and a bullet kicked gravel against the side of his raw face.

'He's down!' a man yelled, and Bighorn recognized the voice as belonging to Mitch Badell.

'If he moves, put the next bullet through him!' called Sawtell, his voice sounding a little further off.

Bighorn gritted his teeth and then saddles creaked and boots crunched on gravel — and one of them slammed into his ribs. The kick almost put him over the trail's edge and he grunted in pain, started to push up with his hands.

He glimpsed Howie Case moving in and then a boot took him under the jaw and his head snapped back and he went out like a candle in a high norther.

'Damn you, Howie!' snapped Sawtell, panting as he came up and pushed Case roughly aside. He glared down at the unconscious Bighorn, then looked across to Mitch Badell. 'All right, you might as well take him while you've got the chance. See that he never comes back to Lazy S.'

Mitch nodded, deadpan, holstered his gun, signed to Howie Case to lend a hand. They were stooping to grab the man under the arms when suddenly Strett was in among them, rifle butt sweeping around. The first blow took Mitch Badell behind the ear and dropped him cold on his face. Before he hit the ground the rifle came arcing back and took Case across the side of the head. He staggered, went down to one knee, a hand barely supporting him. Strett kicked the hand away and clubbed him again, knocking him unconscious.

Sawtell had been taken by complete surprise and his eyes widened when he recognized Strett. Then he snatched at his six-gun while Strett was still turning after clubbing Case.

There was a 'zipping' sound and Sawtell grunted, staggered, dropped his gun and clawed at the flint-tipped arrow shaft that quivered in his chest. He made a choked, surprised sound and dropped to his knees, then back on his heels and finally leaned a shoulder against a boulder, head hanging, blood staining his shirtfront.

Strett snapped his head up, eyes searching. Then he saw her — standing on top of a boulder, her bow in her hand. He knew now why she had made two arrows with stone tips . . .

'You're right — you *do* make good bows and arrows!'

She climbed down silently, went to Sawtell, knocked off his hat and pulled his head up by the hair. For a moment Strett thought she was going to scalp him but then she said in disgust, 'He's still alive!'

'Not for long, I'd guess.' Strett walked across and Sawtell stared at him with dull eyes, his lips framing silent words. Strett brought a canteen and gave the man a drink. Cherokee made an angry sound.

'Why waste it on him? He will soon be dead.'

'And there's no chance of you hurrying things along, is there?'

'Let him die painfully — like my father!'

The dull eyes swivelled to her. 'I never knew your father, lady. You got me . . . mixed-up with someone else . . . '

She slapped him. 'Liar! You were one of the Werewolves! You joined French Pete and Brock and — and Idaho — and the black man in the buckboard — shot my father down where he stood!'

Sawtell shook his head slowly. 'Wrong — '

'You were known as the Canuck,' put in Strett, having an awful feeling rising within him now.

'No. I'm not Canadian: I'm from California. Rainey somehow got the idea that I was from Canada and I never said different . . . it suited me that folks believed I was Canadian.'

Strett got between Cherokee and the dying man. 'How come?'

Sawtell was quiet except for the bubbling sounds of his breathing. He looked up, head moving weakly now. 'I was on the run. Killed my wife in 'Frisco. Her an' her — her lover. Her father was rich — set manhunters on me — I disguised myself as a — a preacher. Stumbled on this wounded man dyin' in the desert. He wanted to make his peace with God, confess his sins. I . . . didn't figure it would hurt. He told me about a lot of crimes, bank robberies and such. He was Canadian and when I asked his name he said . . . said . . . that everyone just called him the Canuck.'

The girl frowned, the angry, disbelieving look on her face slowly ironing-out as Sawtell fought for breath: it was clear he couldn't last much longer.

'This Canuck said he'd killed several people — done time in jail, but it troubled him that he had helped murder a man who had once been his friend — somewhere in Dakota. He . . . called him Red.'

Cherokee's breath hissed between her teeth and she threw the tight-faced

Strett a cold look. 'This sounds very convenient!'

'The man was dying, Cherokee,' Strett told her quietly. 'He needed to unburden his conscience. He mistook Sawtell for a real preacher . . . '

'We only have *his* word for that!' she snapped, but Sawtell, gasping now, hurrying as if he knew he had little time left broke in.

'He said some of those names you . . . just mentioned. Idaho, French Pete. After he died . . . I — I went through his things, found a bag of — of gold and . . . some paper money. A . . . lot.'

It was a struggle for Sawtell to speak now and Strett placed a hand lightly on his arm and said, 'You took that money, used it to buy the Lazy S?' Sawtell stared, eyes dulling now, but his head moved in a slight nod. 'Well, you should never have answered to the name of Canuck, friend. See what it got you . . . ?'

But Sawtell was past caring now. One

hand moved limply, but he couldn't raise it as high as the chest wound. The arrow shaft shuddered, Sawtell's body arched violently — and he died.

The others were still out to it as Cherokee, frowning, turned towards Strett.

'Looks like he was the wrong man, Cherokee.'

Her teeth tugged at her lower lip as she looked down at Sawtell. 'If he spoke the truth then the real Canuck is dead. Now it only leaves the black man — Burns.'

She started to turn away and Strett grabbed her arm roughly, spinning her back to face him, his eyes steely. 'You just killed an innocent man Cherokee!'

'He was *not* innocent! He admitted he killed two people, one of them his own wife! Now he has paid for that crime — if not for the murder of my father!'

Strett shook his head briefly. 'It doesn't work that way.'

She tossed her fiery hair and he

saw the stubborn, brooding look on her face. 'It is done! Nothing can change that!'

Her words silenced him: that was the truth anyway. He looked down at the dead man with the crude arrow still protruding from his chest, and sighed.

'We'd best go find Rainey and see if he really can steer us to this feller Burns — and this time we'd better get it right.'

She was already walking towards her horse and didn't answer him.

10

Last Man Standing

The rendezvous with Tim Rainey was supposed to be in a place called Cowpat Gulch, on Rainey's land, beyond a small hogback with a lone crooked tree growing on it.

But they were passing through a small cutting almost a mile this side of the hogback when suddenly they reined down, saw Rainey sitting a wall-eyed sorrel in the middle of the trail, one heel hooked over the saddlehorn, smoking, relaxed, rubbing up the lenses of his glasses as the cigarette dangled from his thin lips. He smiled crookedly.

'Well, here you are.'

At the same time, Strett heard a movement behind them and started to hip swiftly, snatching at his six-gun. The girl turned, too, already unsheathing her rifle. But they stopped the movements as Mesquite cocked the hammers on the double-barrelled shotgun he held. He didn't speak: nor needed to.

Strett and the girl sat their mounts side by side, instinctively facing Rainey.

'Why's he holding the Greener on us?' Strett asked, jerking his head towards Mesquite.

' 'Cause that's what I told him to do.' Rainey set his glasses on and took one final drag on the cigarette before flicking away the butt. He exhaled the smoke, eyes narrowed as he regarded Strett.

'You don't follow orders good, mister. I told you to drive Sawtell's herd down on to that busted-up country.'

'Just to break their legs?'

'I *wanted* 'em to break their goddamned legs! Not because I got anythin' agin cows — only *Sawtell's* cows! I wanted him to be real upset before you nailed him.'

'He was upset plenty. And Cherokee

201

did nail him. Arrow through the lungs. He didn't die peaceful, if that's anything to brighten your day.'

Rainey smiled thinly. 'Well, it do help some. So, Sawtell's out of it. Now I can move in wherever I want . . . '

Strett frowned, stiffening a little. 'Thought it was the other way around — Sawtell wanting to move in on you.'

Rainey arched his eyebrows, trying to look innocent. 'Wonder where you got that notion . . . ?' He winked. 'Ah, well don't matter. I've kind of had my eyes on some of that canyon country of his, but he's always had too many men for me to try to take it. It ain't part of his spread, just that he kept it by force. Now — Well, I'm beholden to you, Strett, an' the li'l lady, of course.'

'Where can I find the black man?' Cherokee asked singlemindedly.

Again Rainey looked innocent. 'Black man?'

'The one in the buckboard the day he helped kill my father! You said

202

you would tell me where I could find him.'

'Ah, yeah, 'member now. But what I said was, I might be able to give you a *clue* as to where he is . . . ' He sniffed, hawked, spat, shook his head. 'But I've decided it ain't worth worryin' about.'

The girl had stiffened now. 'What does that mean?'

'Means ain't no use me wastin' my breath on telling you somethin' you ain't never gonna use.'

She glanced quickly at Strett who saw the movement of her head only peripherally, concentrating his main attention on Mesquite. He quietly used his knees to turn his horse a little more so that he could see Mesquite more clearly and at the same time keep an eye on Rainey.

'He's gonna kill us, Cherokee,' he said quietly. 'Make himself a local hero, the man who shot down the killers of popular rancher, Sawtell. Clear himself with Cooney and what law there is in these parts, likely have the backing of the town from now on.'

'Good notion, huh?' Rainey sounded pleased with himself.

'Depends where you're sitting,' Strett said and Rainey laughed outright. Mesquite flicked his gaze towards him, instinctively, then Strett's Colt was blazing in his fist.

More by accident than intent, his bullet struck the wide barrels of the Greener and the shotgun spun from Mesquite's grip, exploding as it twirled through the air. The recoil sent the weapon streaking backwards and its butt slammed into Rainey's sorrel's rump. The animal jerked and whinnied and half-reared even as the impact sent it sideways.

Cherokee lunged behind Strett, rammed her horse into Rainey's and sent it all the way down, the rancher with it. Her rifle lever worked swiftly and covered the man as he sprawled on the ground. He looked startled and half-sat up, hands lifted out from his sides.

Mesquite didn't give up so easily: he was a man determined to earn his money. Although shocked by the speed of Strett's draw, his hands tingling from the shotgun wrenching out of his grip, he spurred his mount at Strett's bay. The bay wheeled aside, wrenching its head around, unsettling Strett. He swayed, fighting the reins one-handed, and then Mesquite came hurtling out of the saddle and took him down to the ground where they rolled heavily, both winded as they struggled up.

Strett had dropped his gun, but Mesquite didn't even try for his Colt. He *ran* in, swinging a savage kick at Strett's head as the gunfighter straightened. He took it on the left shoulder, spun with the impact, pain burning down his arm and across his chest. It slowed him down and he didn't quite get his jaw out of the way of Mesquite's haymaker right in time.

Stars exploded before his eyes, his head snapped back and his legs turned into licorice twists. Staggering, dazed,

Strett fought for balance as Mesquite closed, lifting a knee against his hip, hammering at his head and chest. Strett went down and knew through the fog of pain that it was a dangerous place to be with a man like Mesquite moving in with boots swinging.

He rolled but still took a kick beside his spine that almost exploded a kidney. He gagged, twisted on to his back, getting both hands up in front of his face as a boot stamped, downwards. He caught it but it still crushed his hands against his face. But Mesquite lost balance for a moment and Strett knew it was now or never. He heaved, rolled, twisted away, wrenching muscles and that aching spine. But he was clear when Mesquite staggered and one leg folded under him. Strett lurched to his feet, fighting for balance, gritting his teeth against pain as he closed in while the big foreman was still trying to get up.

Strett drove a boot into Mesquite's ribs, moving the man almost a yard across the gravel. As he rolled and tried to get his legs under him, Strett took two running steps and swung another kick that lifted the big man clear off the ground.

He was mighty slow in recovering this time, spat blood, his breath sounding like a buffalo after a stampede. Strett allowed himself time to steady his own breathing, clutching at his chest which pained with each lungful of air he took. Then Mesquite surprised him by letting out a roar and charging in with head down and arms ready to encircle his hips. Strett knew he was finished if he went down again, stepped hurriedly to one side and clubbed a hammerblow against the back of Mesquite's neck. It drove the man face-first into the gravel and, when he staggered up, his face was streaked with blood, small stones and dirt pasted around his eyes and mouth. He spat, clawed his eyes clear and moved in with fists up.

Strett had been waiting for that. He took one step in, feinted with his right, blocked the blow that Mesquite swung on his left forearm, then rammed his right into the other's midriff. Mesquite's legs buckled and he clawed at Strett so as to stay on his feet. Strett moved aside, lifted a knee, the jolting impact straightening the bloody, swaying foreman. Strett measured him with a straight left — and another — and a third — snapping the man's head back each time, blood spraying. The right uppercut travelled from his waist level and brought Mesquite right up to tiptoe. His head seemed to be tilted halfway down his back as his legs folded completely and he sprawled unconscious in the dust . . .

Strett stood there, swaying, feeling the pain of those brutal kicks all over his body. He stumbled to the bay, rinsed his bloody mouth from the canteen, poured more water over his head. He bent down gingerly to pick up his hat, slapped it on his head and walked across to stand beside Cherokee. She stared at him levelly but didn't speak.

She turned to Rainey, poked the rifle barrel against his right kneecap and the man's sucked-in breath was loud in the cutting.

'You have something to tell me?'

Rainey turned his worried gaze to Strett, as if asking, 'Is she really capable of crippling a man . . . ?'

Strett's words were slurred because of his cut and swollen mouth. 'She busted both kneecaps on Brock before shooting a few more bits and pieces out of him, then finally shot him dead when he tried to crawl away.'

'Jesus!' Rainey breathed the word like prayer. He had lost some colour, as he looked up at the unsmiling girl. 'Look — it's just somethin' I picked up from a feller I had workin' for me last round-up. He'd come down from Iowa, a little place called Red Oak. Happened to speak about a crippled Negro married to a white woman, how the town's finally accepted 'em since they sort of help folk in trouble — ex-convicts, women, kids . . . '

Cherokee frowned. 'This is Burns?'

'Well, it could be. When I was still a lawman we heard that Salty Burns had taken a shotgun blast in one hip and would never walk much again — which could explain why he never got outa that buckboard when you saw him with the men who killed your pa, li'l lady. That's all I know. But I think it could be Burns. Most everyone knew he married a white do-gooder when he got outa Yuma.'

She glanced at Strett and he nodded. 'Seems pretty good — and Iowa's not all that far.'

She held his gaze for a few moments, looked down at Rainey. 'You were going to kill us both.'

He flinched and lost more colour at her casual tone, forced a short laugh. 'Well, guess there's no use denyin' it, eh? But it all worked out OK. You ride out and never come this way again and you got nothin' to worry about, right?'

'Mmm. But I think you should let

people think you put up some kind of fight to stop us — escaping,' she said.

Strett caught the well-known flash of anticipation in her eyes and said, quickly, 'Don't, Cherokee!'

The crash of the rifle drowned his protest — and Tim Rainey's scream.

* * *

They took stage coaches and trains to Iowa, left the last train at Omaha, Nebraska, and bought horses and supplies and rode the rest of the way to Red Oak.

It was a bigger town than Strett expected and he said so to Cherokee but she only shrugged. There hadn't been much conversation on the way up from Rawlins: she had seemed to prefer her own thoughts, whatever they were.

They asked directions and next day rode out to the farm where a gang of men were working the bottom-land along a creek. They stopped work to lean on their shovels and stare at the girl. It didn't appear to bother her.

Not even when one man cat-called, 'I just died an' seen an angel!' Their manner, coupled with their sallow colour and the way they spoke out of the sides of their mouths and their suspicious eyes, told Strett that these were ex-jailbirds. Likely some of Burns's recruits for his rehabilitation scheme.

'Anyone at home?' Strett asked, but only got blank, dumb-insolent stares by way of reply.

They rode on towards the small farmhouse, past the long bunkhouse and dismounted at the steps leading to the porch.

The door opened and a small woman in her late forties appeared, smiling with large teeth, pushing a strand of string-coloured hair back beneath the edge of the bandanna tied about her head. She was a plain woman, but her smile was warm and genuinely welcoming. She stepped to the edge of the porch. 'Why, what a pleasant surprise! Visitors on such a lovely day!'

Strett smiled politely as he touched a hand to his hat-brim. Cherokee's face was impassive as she said directly, 'We wish to see Mr Burns.'

The woman's smile tightened just a tad as she blinked. 'I'm sorry, this is the Mason place: Mr and Mrs Lute Mason?'

'His name is 'Salty' Burns and he — '

'We would like to see your husband, ma'am,' Strett cut in, 'whatever name he goes by now.'

Aggie Mason's smile had all but disappeared now. But she was putting a brave face on it, studying her visitors much more closely now. 'He's a'bed.'

'Yes'm, we figured he might be.'

Aggie's mouth tightened. 'So — you already know he is crippled. May I ask your names?'

'I'm Walker Strett and this is — '

'Cherokee McKenna! *Red* McKenna's daughter!' The buckskin girl's eyes

213

burned into Aggie Mason who put a hand to her mouth. 'Tell your husband *that*!'

But Aggie held on to her composure and Strett admired the way she did it, knowing this moment must have been one hell of a shock for her. 'I — I know little of Mr McKenna, but as I understood it he did not have any . . . children.'

'*I* am his daughter!' Cherokee said firmly as she started up the steps. 'I want to see your husband.'

Strett, afraid Cherokee was going to use brute force on the other woman, reached for her, but she merely stood in front of Aggie, waiting. The Mason woman was afraid but trying not to show it. She looked past Cherokee to the fields where the men were still leaning on their tools, watching.

'I only need to signal that I need help and they will come,' she said quietly.

'Let's just talk with your husband, ma'am. We only want to clear up a few things.'

Strett sounded reasonable and Aggie Mason hesitated, then moved aside and gestured for them to enter the house. They stepped into a neat parlour with a crucifix above the fireplace and framed, embroidered texts from the Bible and the Psalms scattered about the walls. The floors were clean, the rugs colourful and obviously hand-made.

Aggie led the way down a short passage to a rear bedroom. There was a black man propped up in the iron-framed bed, books and papers scattered about him on the covers, piled high on the straightback chair beside the bed. He glanced up at his wife as she ushered in the visitors and introduced them.

His face was sunken, the dark, leathery skin giving him a mummified look. Strett knew here was a man who had endured unending pain for many years. Mason's teeth tugged at a corner of his purplish bottom lip as he looked at Cherokee.

'McKenna . . . ? I heard Red was married to a part-Indian woman but I never knew he had any children.'

'So you admit you knew my father?'

'Oh, yes, I knew Red — very well, in fact. And I know why you're here. I've been kind of expecting you since I heard about the deaths of Brock and French Pete. Are there any more I should add to the list?'

Cherokee was frowning now, obviously thrown out of step by Mason — or Burns — in his open approach.

'The Canuck!' She tried to make her voice vicious but the black man frowned. 'Add him! Or tell me where he is!'

'But he died years ago — in the Mojave Desert, I heard. If you've killed someone you believed was him, it's a terrible mistake!'

She flushed, surprising Strett, who said, carefully, 'Then, it was because we were given a bum steer. Same feller told us about Idaho, too — and you.'

Mason's wrinkled face was very sober

now. 'I . . . see.' He glanced at his wife and smiled — only it didn't quite come off and Strett figured the man was still in a lot of pain — a *lot* of pain.

'It's all right, my dear,' Mason said to Aggie. 'You know I've had a bad conscience all these years. I'll feel better when I get it said.'

She moved swiftly to his side, hitched a small buttock on to the edge of the mattress and took one of her husband's hands between hers. Her look was quite defiant as she flicked her gaze from Strett to Cherokee.

Mason spoke quietly in an easy-sounding voice. 'Cherokee, I expect you're here to take revenge for your pa's killing — I guess it has to be that. Well, I must tell you a story. I'll be as brief as I can. Mr Strett, I know you by reputation. Have you ever asked yourself *why* five men would ride hundreds of miles after spending years tracking down a particular man — and risk everything by riding in openly to kill that man?'

'I've thought about it some,' Strett admitted and glanced at the girl. 'But I never pursued it.'

Mason arched his eyebrows. 'Sensitivity in a man such as you, Mr Strett? I am impressed.'

'What are you saying about my father?' Cherokee demanded impatiently.

Mason sighed. 'You won't like this, I'm afraid, Cherokee, but it must be said. No doubt you know your father rode with our bunch. We called ourselves the Werewolves for no good reason. We broke all the laws of the land, robbed and occasionally killed when we had to. Naturally, we were fired upon and most of us were wounded at one time or another.

'When Red was hit, it was in the head — here — just above the left temple. He very nearly died . . . '

'Yes, my father did have a scar in that place,' Cherokee said softly, and Mason nodded, continued.

'He recovered, but that wound affected him — well, badly. He became trigger-happy, killing at the least provocation, until we no longer wanted him in our gang.'

'You lie, black man!' Cherokee hissed, shaking now. Strett quickly laid a hand on her arm.

'Child, I have been a practising Christian for many years now — I've told all the lies I'm ever going to tell. You can believe that what I say now is the truth. It may hurt, and I'm truly sorry but — Your father, for a time I stress, was like a mad dog. He gave us all a very bad reputation and then, perhaps sensing we were turning against him, he sold us out to the law.'

She was white now, the high cheek-bones much more prominent than usual, eyes smouldering. But she remained quiet.

'Yes, he sold us out in return for immunity and a handful of dollars. The law was waiting for us when we went to pull what was to have been our biggest — and last job. Somehow we escaped, but three of us were wounded.' He indicated his hip. 'I was the worst hit. Afterwards, we broke up, went our separate ways — some of us to jail under other names. But we all swore one day we'd have our revenge on McKenna.'

The words trailed off and Cherokee hissed, 'You murdered a good man! He was nothing like you say! He was *good*! The best of fathers to me, kind to Sun Flower, the Comanche woman he took to live with him so she could care for me. And you — you helped *murder* this good man!'

Strett dug his fingers into her arm, feeling her tension, her anger trembling through her. Mason nodded sadly at her accusation. 'Yes. We were too eager, never took the time to see if the years had changed him. We never allowed that he *might* change, that the blood clot or whatever it was that made him an insane killer would one day heal over — and he would be the old Red we had known — a practical joker, a man who would give you his last few flakes of tobacco or his last dollar, a man who would rather knock a bank guard cold than shoot him. Oh, he wasn't a law-abiding type, but before that terrible wound Red McKenna had been a likeable *man* — and we never for a moment thought he would ever return to that kind of person, that he would recover, from the influence of that head-wound. I am terribly sorry, my dear, but we being the men we were and leading the kind of life we did at that time . . . '

Strett was expecting her to reach for her pistol and shoot Mason any instant. She struggled against his grip but he knew her heart wasn't in it. Her mind was occupied with something else. This ailing black man had a way of speaking that allowed the listener to *feel* his sincerity and, Strett wondered, dared to *hope* even, that Cherokee, too, could feel this — repentance — that gripped Lute Mason, alias Salty Burns. Her mind must be a whirlpool right now.

'Child, I dislike having to tell you this about your father. Obviously it all happened in a life before you knew him. It is fitting that you remember him the way he was with you. I ask your forgiveness as I have asked God's these many years, but if I should have to die by your hand, I know it will be the only way I can atone for my sins in the Lord's eyes.'

'You *will* die for killing my father!' Cherokee said very quietly, and Strett sank his fingers hard enough into her arm to make her wince. She snapped her head around towards him, angrily.

'Cherokee, I think you should leave this one. Kind of balance the books, make up for Sawtell.'

'I do not need you any more, Walker Strett! I do not need your advice!'

She looked wild, but he thought that the most dangerous moment had passed. If she really meant to kill Mason, she would have done it already. *And* his wife . . .

'It's been a long time, Cherokee,' he

told her gently. 'You've avenged your father. You found and killed Brock and French Pete. The Canuck is dead and so is Idaho — and Burns here — well, surely he's suffered enough to satisfy you.'

'Vengeance is the business of the Good Lord only, Cherokee,' Mrs Mason said in a strained voice. 'We beseech you . . .'

'Don't beg!' Cherokee snapped. 'I have lived more than half my life as a Comanche. We detest cowardice in friend *or* enemy!'

Mason seemed to draw himself up in the bed, his arm going around his wife's shoulders. There was a strange dignity about him when he spoke. 'Cherokee, we are at your mercy but we are not afraid. We have our faith and know that another, better life awaits us. It is the state of *your* soul that concerns us.'

Strett sensed she was confused, torn between her innate decency that urged her to accept this man's repentance, and the desire to spill blood in the Comanche way, as the *only* way of wiping out a debt of this magnitude.

'Cherokee,' he said quietly. 'Leave it. He's the last one. He's done his best to atone for a lot of things. Give him his chance.'

She looked back at the Masons. Her hand strayed towards her gun.

The black man, more uneasy than he allowed to show, cleared his throat and asked Strett, 'Who told you that Idaho was dead?'

'Man named Rainey. Said Idaho drowned in '74.'

Mason slowly shook his head. He had their attention now. 'One of the men I rehabilitated knew Idaho. Claimed the man now owns a ranch in Wyoming. This was around 1880. He said that Idaho now wears spectacles and that was what made me believe him, because Idaho had been having trouble with his eyesight for a very long time when I knew him . . . '

'Rainey!' breathed the gunfighter.

Cherokee snapped her head towards Strett. 'Rainey said Burns never got out of the buckboard the day my father was killed! But I never mentioned that!' She swung back towards Mason. 'I was watching from the cabin. You *didn't* leave the buckboard, did you?'

'That's right, child — I can't even climb out of bed without help.'

'The only way Rainey could know you never left the buckboard was if he was there and saw it!'

Strett nodded. 'Yeah — I think you're right. Rainey is Idaho Reese.'

★ ★ ★

It was weeks since they had left Rainey's spread and Strett wondered how they were going to get past the hardcases the man employed. A crippled Rainey would be guarded more tightly than ever. But he needn't have worried.

Because Rainey wasn't about to let a shattered kneecap keep him from squaring things with the person who

225

had done it to him.

He'd blow Strett's head off, too, if ever they crossed trails again. But nothing would stop him going after that buckskin gal!

Also, Mesquite was having trouble coming to terms with the knowledge that he had been beaten to a pulp by Walker Strett. No man in all of Wyoming Territory had even knocked him off his feet, let alone hammered him into such a bloody wreck. Some of his ribs were cracked and he spent some time in Doc Moses' infirmary in Rawlins, next bed to Rainey.

The rancher would be lucky to ever walk again without the aid of a crutch. At best he would always have to use a walking stick to help support his leg with the shattered knee cap. It would be a lifetime reminder of what a slip of a half-breed girl in buckskin had done to Tim Rainey.

When Mesquite told his boss he was quitting and going to Red Oak, Iowa, to find Strett, Rainey, looking thinner and much drawn, said, 'Wait up Mesquite. Gimme a coupla more days to get this goddamn plaster cast off an' I'll come with you.'

'Don't need no help in this, boss.'

'I got me an account to settle with that damn squaw. Thousand bucks, an' you're on the payroll permanent. What d'ya say?'

That did it, and two weeks later they left Rawlins, Mesquite forking a thick-legged buckskin, while Rainey cussed and sweated over a double-teamed buckboard, crutches in the back, a bottle of red-eye 'painkiller' in his lap.

* * *

The girl had been very quiet since leaving Red Oak. Strett knew she was still wondering if she had done the right thing, leaving Salty Burns — alias Lute Mason — alive. But he figured this was something she had to come to terms with herself. There wasn't anything he could say that would help. Though, if later she changed her mind — well, he would do his best to stop her. *He* figured Burns had paid his debt.

Her mind must be a hurricane of thoughts and emotions. The image she had held of her father had been tarnished considerably and yet she must have believed Burns's version or she would never have left him alive.

She was maybe a lot more mature than he had so far given her credit for: in any case, the problem was hers. She had said no more about not needing Strett any more but it wouldn't have made any difference. He would tag along now, to the very end, see her through this. One way or another: to the very end . . .

He knew she had never given any thought to the possibility that she might be killed. Personally, he did not aim to underrate Rainey.

And yet he did. Because he was totally unprepared when they rounded a bend in the foothills of the Laramie

Mountains and found the buckboard blocking their trail, Rainey half-sprawled across the front seat, menacing them with a cocked shotgun.

As Strett instinctively started to reach for his Colt, Mesquite's heavy voice behind them warned, 'Leave it be, gunfighter! Just set — just — *set*!' He held a cocked rifle and his scarred face was twisted in a half-grin, as he watched the shock hit Strett and the girl. 'You an' me, we got us a reckonin' comin', Strett!'

'And you an' *me*, darlin'!' grated Rainey viciously to Cherokee, his words a mite slurred. 'An, it's gonna be one that'll last a long, long time before you go to your happy huntin' grounds, you squaw bitch!'

The girl's expression didn't change, but her eyes were narrowed. 'I know who you are — Idaho!'

Rainey laughed. 'Yeah, that's me. No matter now. You kill ol' Salty?'

She didn't reply, let him make up his own mind.

'Whooo-eeee! You are one mean bitch! Hey, Mesquite, I'm gonna really enjoy this!' He jerked the gun at the girl but she didn't move. He scowled. 'Don't think just because I only got one good leg it'll stop me from doin' everythin' I want with you! Doc Moses gimme a book about crippled folk an' how they get along in married life. I'm kinda lookin' forward to tryin' some of them things . . . '

He shifted his mocking gaze to Strett. 'You — you're all Mesquite's. He'll keep you outa my hair while me and Miss Buckskin make our own fun. Right, Mesquite?'

'He won't bother you none,' the big man assured him.

'Tell me one thing, Rainey.' Strett spoke quickly, trying to delay things for as long as he could. Even seconds could count in a situation like this. 'Why'd you tell everyone Sawtell was the Canuck?'

'Figured it wouldn't hurt, seein' as he was claimin' to come from Canada,

230

anyways. Then after I heard about French Pete and Brock, I got me a queer feelin' in the belly. Seemed to me that someone was on a vengeance trail, after all these years. I ain't lived as long as I have by takin' chances so when you two showed and told your story, I thought up that bit about the Werewolves — as a kinda test.' He shook his head slowly. 'Could hardly believe a little thing like that gal could be so much of a devil. Me, I was where I wanted to be, had big plans, so I figured I'd best divert attention from myself and, seein' as Sawtell had a lot more men than me, I figured to steer you to him and let you get rid of him for me.'

'Thoughtful of you,' opined Strett, trying to keep the man talking, but Idaho had his own schedule and said, 'Never figured you'd have a chance to use that bit I told you about Salty Burns. Then, *she* goes and blows off my kneecap!' His eyes blazed behind the spectacles at the girl. 'Now you climb on down, you bitch, and *crawl* over here! *Right now, damn you!*'

Strett stirred and that was all the excuse Mesquite needed. The foreman spurred his mount forward, smashing it into Strett's mount, a dappled grey. It went down whinnying and Strett jumped clear, landing on hands and knees. Mesquite spurred his buckskin at him, knocking him back several feet. Strett kept rolling as the horse tried to trample him. He spun, kicked away, threw up his arms, took a hoof heavily on the shoulder. Mesquite yelled triumphantly, tried to smash Strett flat, but the man shoulder-rolled, coming up on to one knee, clawing dust from his eyes with his left hand, right sweeping up the six-gun from his holster in a blurring draw.

Mesquite was still on the rearing horse when the gun blazed in two fast shots. The big man was blown clear out of the saddle. He hit hard, rolled, an arm flopped, and Strett thought he was trying for his gun and shot him again. He could have saved his lead — the first two had done the job.

Still kneeling in the dust he swung towards Rainey who only now fired the shotgun. Strett twisted as buckshot peppered his upper right arm and his smoking six-gun fell from his grip. He grabbed the arm, blood oozing as Rainey swung up the gun for the second shot.

Something flashed through the air and Rainey grunted and straightened up awkwardly. But his bad leg wouldn't hold him and he tumbled forward over the buckboard side, the shotgun thundering as he hit the dust. He flopped on to his back and through the pain blurring his vision, Strett saw Cherokee's knife protruding from just beneath Rainey's throat.

Then he swayed and fell sideways, twisting so as not to land on his wounded gun arm . . .

She was kneeling beside him, pouring water into the six shot-wounds, when he came back to reality. He sucked in a sharp breath as the water stung.

'I have dug out the shot,' she told him. 'Your arm seems to be . . . damaged,' she added as she began to bandage it.

He nodded slowly. 'Can't move my fingers too well. Middle one feels kind of numb. So does my hand. Something must've been cut, a tendon or a nerve.'

'I will take you to a doctor.'

'Can't go near Rawlins,' he warned.

Cherokee smiled thinly. 'I know a doctor. It is a long way but he . . . I have seen him perform miracles.'

Strett snapped his head up.

'My tribe's shaman. He is Sun Flower's uncle. He will make your arm work again. It may be long and painful, but he will do it.'

Strett looked dubious.

'He *will*!' she assured him. 'Anyway, you will have a chance to meet my son. He can show you the Indian ways while you are getting better.'

Strett thought about it. But not for long.

'Well, I sure need this arm . . . and I'd be honoured to meet your son, Cherokee.'

She gave him the first truly warm and relaxed smile he had seen and it transformed her face into something lovely — 'proud' was the only word that came to mind. He knew then she had come to terms with her devils. She might take a little more time settling down, but she *would* do it.

Now she looked at him with a gentleness in her eyes he had never seen before. She spoke very quietly.

'I was wrong, Walker, when I said I do not need you any more . . . '

He smiled. 'That's OK. I always figured to come a'running if ever you needed me. You can still count on that.'

Again that warm smile, transforming her face. 'Yes. I think I knew that all along. You are a man to be counted on, Walker Strett.'

THE BOUNTYMEN

Tom Anson

Tom Quinlan headed a bunch of other bounty hunters to bring in the long-sought Dave Cull, who was not expected to be alone. That they would face difficulties was clear, but an added complication was the attitude of Quinlan's strong-minded woman, Belle. And suddenly, mixed up in the search for Cull, was the dangerous Arn Lazarus and his men. Hunters and hunted were soon embroiled in a deadly game whose outcome none could predict.

THE EARLY LYNCHING

Mark Bannerman

Young Rice Sheridan leaves behind his adoptive Comanche parents and finds work on the Double Star Ranch. Three years later, he and his boss, Seth Early, are ambushed by outlaws, and their leader, the formidable Vince Corby, brutally murders Early. Rice survives and reaches town. Pitched into a maelstrom of deception and treachery, Rice is nevertheless determined that nothing will prevent him from taking revenge on Corby. But he faces death at every turn . . .

RENEGADE BLOOD

Johnny Mack Bride

Joe Gage was a drifter who'd never had a regular job until, in Dearman, Colorado, he found steady work and met a pretty girl. But he also fell foul of the feared Hunsen clan, a family of mad, murderous renegades who decided he was their enemy. Joe had two choices: give up his future and ride out of the territory, or fight against the 'Family from Hell'. He made his decision, but he was just one man against many.

RIO REPRISAL

Jake Douglas

Life had taken on a new meaning for Jordan and all he wanted was to be left alone, but it was not to be. Back home, there were only blackened ruins and Mandy had been taken by the feared Apache, Wolf Taker. The only men Jordan could turn to for help were the outlaws with whom he had once ridden, but their price was high and bloody. Nevertheless, Jordan was prepared to tear the entire southwest apart as long as he found Mandy.

DEATH MARCH IN MONTANA

Bill Foord

Held under armed guard in a Union prison camp, Captain Pat Quaid learns that the beautiful wife of the sadistic commandant wants her husband killed. She engineers the escape of Quaid and his young friend Billy Childs in exchange for Quaid's promise to turn hired gunman. He has reasons enough to carry out the promise, but he's never shot a man in cold blood. Can he do it for revenge, hatred or love?

A LAND TO DIE FOR

Tyler Hatch

There were two big ranches in the valley: Box T and Flag. Ben Tanner's Box T was the larger and he ran things his way. Wes Flag seemed content to play second fiddle to Tanner — until he married Shirley. But the trouble hit the valley and soon everyone was involved. Now it was all down to Tanner's loyal ramrod, Jesse McCord. He had to face some tough decisions if he was to bring peace to the troubled range — and come out alive.